The Shadow and The Stag

By David J. Neumaier

First printed in the United States of America

First hardback edition December 2025

Cover Design by Matthew P. Smyser and David J. Neumaier

ISBN (Hardback): 979-8-9875739-5-2
ISBN (Paperback): 979-8-9875739-4-5
ISBN (Kindle): 979-8-9875739-3-8

www.davidjneumaier.com

For those who helped make me,
for Him who saved me,
and to all who suffer

Prologue

The days of Man are numbered. And in the time when the cruel actusfie had newly rebelled against their maker, those days were few. In the eyes of Man, the world lacked color. It lacked meaning. All that was understood were the harsh realities of pain and death and warfare. Man found it was easier to take than it was to make. To use than to love. To act rather than reflect.

Pain was the result of Man's own actions. His own weaknesses. If pain came, it was never the fault of another. Man was not responsible for any man beyond himself. Helplessness against pain fueled the rage which clouded the mind of Man.

But Man was not made for such shallow ends. Man was made to make, to love, and reflect. Serinth, the Maker, sought to renew Man's end.

First, Serinth sent the axuli, creatures of love and life, veiled as ordinary beasts in the young world. They took the form of docile prey; rabbits, deer, horses, and birds, so that Man would pursue them. In return, the axuli, Serinth's friends, offered protection from the actusfie, so long as Man was willing to receive it.

Gradually, in Man's pursuits of axuli, clarity prevailed in the minds of the men. These clear-minded men became leaders, guides that would communicate with the axuli to find food and water. Most importantly, the wisdom of the axuli brought Man peace. Small tribes formed around these leaders who called themselves "Shamans."

But while Man could still be divided, the actusfie would continue their hunts. As Man organized himself, the actusfie organized themselves, too. The actusfie formed legions of spirits in the forms of wolves, bears, coyotes, cougars, and some as dark clouds. Some claimed the corpses of Man, victims of their ill will.

Serinth, however, had not abandoned his creation. The axuli stood as guardians for mankind, but Man still lacked unity. Serinth offered it.

Appearing in the form of a brilliant white stag, shining through the dark of night and the bright of day as a beacon of hope, Serinth brought Man unto himself. He led them on a long journey through the woods, ever silent and ever watchful, until they came to an open plain beside a trio of mountains, with a fresh, full river and hope.

Serinth led mankind into the valley between the three mountains, set there solely for Man, and watched over them as they made their residence, Som Catre, the Quiet Mountains. The actusfie feared the presence of Serinth and kept their distance, waiting for the moment when chaos and pain could be renewed. Waiting for the moment when Serinth would inevitably leave Man alone, cornered in the mountain valley.

But Serinth would never leave Man. When the city was built, Serinth, silent as ever, stepped beyond its gates and no man, woman or child dared to ask why. The brilliant white stag drifted into the Aiman, the common source of all the water on the continent of Retaran, and lay itself down.

The water washed Serinth away, taking his power upon itself. But the actusfie did not understand this and began their approach. The fallen spirits charged toward the Quiet Mountains.

Yet when the first few of these rebellious spirits touched the water, they vanished into ash and smoke.

Winter's Edge

It was a quiet morning in Lagdin Village. The dense woods that surrounded it were still dark within for the most part but the rising sunlight would soon scatter on the ground through the leaves. A small stream trickled by the western side of the village, running from the north where the mountains and great river of Aiman lie. The capital of Retaran, Som Catre, was nothing more than a distant dream to the villagers. Many were still asleep, as they should have been, and those that weren't were rekindling the hearth, the pops and cracks of wood breaking the still morning silence.

A thin layer of snow carpeted the ground outside each door and upon every rooftop. The first snowfall of the winter. In every home, there was a small surplus of carrots, potatoes, squash and pumpkins gathered meticulously from their gardens to last them through the season.

The village was circular. A sharp-pointed wooden fence with the occasional shaman-made charm protected the people from the threats of the forest. The ring of houses bordering the fence were filled mostly with single men deemed by the shaman to be strong enough to serve as sentries to watch for particularly evil things that prowled in the surrounding forest. Evil things that loved to lure the weak-willed children beyond the safety of their village. The inner ring of the village contained families that managed everything from cooking and building to crafting and gardening. Near the center of the village, traveling traders would sell their goods.

The traders would come from all over the kingdom. Those that could afford the costs of travel to Lagdin carried luxury goods that the men would use as gifts during courtship. There was no other way to guarantee a profit. The irregular climate, distance, and dangers on the road drove up the costs. So few traders visited.

It was the time when families began their morning chores to make time for afternoon relaxation or, in the case of children, play.

"Alechi, come help me with this firewood," a father said to his son. They were outside the village within a stone's throw of the eastern entrance. Many families were around the area preparing firewood for the rest of the day. Alechi and his father worked quickly before dawn and got to chopping wood. Within an hour of work, they had split enough between the two of them for a whole day for two households: one for their own and one for an assigned guard house, as per custom.

Alechi was rather tall, though not yet taller than his father, he had blueish-green eyes and short brown hair. He was the oldest of his father's children—aged about thirteen winters. His hands were raw from working with an ax so early in the morning in the cold. He was still young, but not young enough to enjoy the luxury of irresponsibility.

His father placed covers on their axes. Alechi bundled the wood and the axes with rope, strapped it over his shoulders, then walked past the heavily armed guards at the entrance, their eyes peeled for any unwelcome that dared to approach from the woods. The guards paid him no heed.

Just then, a small hunting party that had stayed the night in the forest, much to the disapproval of Lagdin's shaman, broke through the trees, strolling carelessly toward the eastern gate. A few carried spears that doubled as walking sticks, and others slung bows over their shoulders with a quiver at their belt. Strangely, they were joined by a pair of seemingly tame, young wolves. Alechi's father stiffened and ushered his son away from the gate, telling him to take the bundle he carried to the guard house. Lifting the bundle on his back a little higher, Alechi made his way to the north side of the village. His father made his way back to their home without looking back.

The wolves had black fur that was long enough to hide the eyes from any distant viewer, but the slow rotations of the wolves' heads indicated that they were searching for something.

The guards at the gate dropped to a knee and braced their spears against the hard earth.

The village shaman was standing over the eastern gate. Scattering the birds from their branches, his voice shook the trees as he spoke, "What do you think you are doing?"

The hunting party stopped in their tracks, but the wolves continued their slow prowl forward.

"Come on, shaman," one of the hunting members complained.

"Can't you see these ones are harmless? Give 'em a little meat from a kill and they'll do anything you say!"

"It isn't my rule. It's Serinth's. Rules have reasons," he responded, his eyebrows furrowing. "Guards!" Then he and a pair of guards descended from atop the gate to stand between the posts, forming a line with the other spearmen. Nothing happened for a few moments. Then, taking notice of the shaman's presence, the pair of wolves growled. They bounded forward, snapping their fierce jaws.

"No!" one of the hunters called out, finally realizing his mistake. He dashed forward but tripped over his own feet.

The guards on the outer flank of the shaman stopped the wolves, their spears taking the brunt of the charge as the point slipped into to the beasts' rib cages. With a surge of strength, the other pair guards pushed forward and arced their spears to pin the wolves to the ground. The shaman started with the one on his right. As he moved his hand toward it, its ferocious gnashing weakened to a whimper, and with little effort, the shaman's hand pushed the wolf to the ground. He said a simple spell under his breath, and the wolf faded to ash. He then repeated it for the other, and it too faded to ash.

The shaman walked to the fallen member of the distraught hunting party and offered a hand. He repeated, "Rules have reasons."

Alechi turned his head when he heard the commotion at the gate, but saw nothing he could understand. He resumed his walk to the guardhouse. When Alechi arrived at his destination, he placed the bundle of wood on the doorstep, knocked twice and took a step back. A strong man about the age of Alechi's father opened the door and nodded once he saw the wood on the doorstep. Alechi was doing his best in hiding the fact that his hands were cold and bowed graciously before the guard, turned to leave. After he had taken a few steps, he could no longer stand his freezing fingertips. He tried to first to shake them free of the cold. When that failed, he rubbed his hands together and drew them close to his warm breath.

"Alechi!" The guard called out, noticing the boy's red face and fingertips, "Come inside for a moment. You've earned the warmth. The sun's still not showing its full face quite yet; you can spare a moment and wait for it to warm up."

"I really shouldn't, I need to help my father with some other preparations for the winter. We want to reinforce the roof so that the snow doesn't cave in on us while we are sleeping like it did last winter."

The guard laughed. "I remember that! Bah, it won't take long. Jerald can wait! And if he can't, I will help reinforce the roof myself later."

"You have a job to do too, Calius," Alechi reminded him. "The shaman would not be pleased to hear you are slacking off."

Calius smiled, pointing his finger, "Especially if he knew you were the cause."

"You are the one asking me to come in."

"And you are the one refusing." His grin extended. "Oh fine, go off and help your father. Thank you again for the wood!"

"Only doing my duty, Calius," Alechi responded. "Now get back to yours before I tell the shaman you slowed me, my father, and yourself down."

"Oooh... *Scary...*" Calius said before waving goodbye and bringing the wood inside the guardhouse. Alechi turned away again from the guardhouse and jogged back to his home a few rings inward from the outer ring. He wanted to keep warm but also reserve his energy for the hammering on the roof. Though it was only near the beginning of winter, the already-thin air sapped the strength of his lungs.

He arrived in front of his house, stomped his feet to rid himself of the early morning frost that clung desperately to the soles of his boots, opened the door and was welcomed by his father with a cup of hot water. "What took you so long?" his father asked him quietly as younger members of the family were still asleep.

"Calius held me up," he explained. He sipped from the wooden cup slowly as the water would still scald his tongue on occasion if he was not careful.

"Nothing new up there I see," his father smiled. "Sure you do not want to try tea again?"

Alechi recalled the drink's bitter taste and with an exaggeration of disgust confirmed, "I'm sure." The two of them sat by the fire and breathed the warm air with a sense of serenity and calm. Once his father had finished his tea, he placed the cup face down on a wooden plate a short distance from the fire to keep it warm. Alechi did the same. The firelight danced on the windowless walls. Its mellow, orange flame was attractive compared to the cold gray that awaited them outside. The warmth of the hearth seeped into their bones, inviting them back to sleep, but a crack from a falling log snapped Alechi out of the trance. "Should we get started?" he suggested.

"Yes, of course," his father said, escaping his own trance.

Behind the house, they kept the wood they had cut down from two trees in the forest to use for additional support for the roof. The collapse happened near the end of winter. By the time they finished the repairs in early spring, it hardly seemed worth immediately reinforcing. Rain had never been a problem for them, so they did not worry about it.

Ever since, Alechi took upon himself more responsibilities in helping his family. It was then that he started assisting with the firewood early on but soon started helping with the hunting and cooking as well. The next oldest of his siblings, Beth, was still three years behind him, so he would be helping his father with these tasks without much leave. Casey, the next oldest son, was six years his younger, and Dailyn, the youngest daughter, was five this spring.

Being the nimbler of the pair, Alechi climbed up onto the roof and removed the hay that caught most of the water so that he could access the wooden frame underneath. Fortunately, nothing was broken, so he spent the day coordinating with his father how to best utilize the new wood. Once they decided, Alechi was up and down the whole day. His father handled most of the lifting, and Alechi was responsible for putting the hay back on top once they were done. By the end of it all, he was exhausted. He wanted nothing more than to go back to playing in the markets and taunting the guards like he did not even a full year ago. But tomorrow was going to be busy as well— the town was set to start another hunt for the larger game before they went into hibernation for the season.

2

The Boast

Day fell, night passed, and the morning routine resumed as usual. Alechi escaped the delay this time as even Calius knew today was the last hunt before winter. They would trap smaller game during the season itself, but it was inconsistent as all rabbits had to be brought before the shaman to check if it was an axuli, thus potentially wasting bait and a trap. Multiple families grouped up to take responsibility for different parts of the forest. There was safety and efficiency in numbers.

Alechi's father, Jerald, handed him a dagger to use as his father would use the bow. "Don't let go of this dagger," he told him. "And don't use it unless I tell you to." Alechi nodded in understanding. The village expected them to come back with at least one stag per family; Jerald, however, was known for being able to secure at least two if not three stags on his own every season. He was a sure shot even in the dark woods and unbelievably quiet when he wanted to be. Jerald claimed it was always just luck, or that more stags roamed near the eastern edge where he hunted, but the whole village agreed it was skill. Today was the first time in three winters he would work with someone else. And that someone was his son. Understandably, the whole village was anxious to see how many they could bring back this year.

In the early morning, the gray of dawn had not quite been shattered by the sun as Jerald and Alechi made their first outing. They had worked out hand signals with each other for various purposes ranging from "stag spotted, quiet" to "watch where you step."

It did not take long for them to find their first set of tracks. The ground was still wet and impressionable from the dewy morning. They followed a trail until they came to an open glade with a single sizable stone in the middle where a large stag grazed on some of the grass on the far edge still within the protection of the trees. Its head was sticking out which was enough for Jerald to kill. The wind was in their favor, the stag had not scented them. Alechi held up his index and little finger by the side of his face then moved it slowly to his lips, practicing the sign developed for, "Stag spotted, quiet." Alechi refused to even breathe and watched patiently as his father took one slow breath, drawing the bow back and aiming with both of his eyes to shoot. After what seemed like an eternity of silence, he released his arrow. With a quiet but secure *thud* the arrow was embedded in the stag's skull, directly between its antlers. Its legs buckled, and the animal collapsed where it stood. Alechi and his father snuck toward the stag as the last of the light of life faded from its eyes. Jerald motioned to draw the knife and slit the stag's neck. Just to be sure. It made no movement at the pain of the knife certifying its death. Jerald spoke first, "Good job, I'm surprised you were able to stay quiet for so long while we followed its trail. Good eye."

"Thank you," Alechi said, smiling wide.

"Let's get this one back home, we still have plenty of daylight ahead of us." Jerald led the way back through the forest, the dead stag secured to his back. Alechi carried the bow, quiver, and the dagger in his stead. As the first ones to return with a stag, they were praised for their speed and for the size of the stag they brought. They gave it to the town butcher to prepare for their family while they went back out to hunt. By the end of the day, they had brought back three stags in total and a pair of fat rabbits that were caught in the traplines and placed before the shaman.

The shaman addressed the rabbits with the utmost respect and looked carefully into their eyes. Alechi could have sworn the shaman was communicating with them. The grayish-brown rabbit was observed and passed over easily. The other rabbit, also brown but with a distinctive light gray spot on its left leg, however, took more time. After a few mysteriously silent moments, the shaman nodded to the rabbit with an understanding look.

"This one cannot be eaten," the shaman said definitively. "Release it back into the forest when you set the traps again. It is not this one's time. The fully brown one you may take to your home and eat."

"Why not?" Alechi asked. It was his first time seeing such a ritual.

"You may understand in due time, but for now just know this

one is not quite ready."

"But-"

"We understand, shaman," Jerald interrupted. Then he led his son to the eastern edge of the village with the rabbit in his arms. It seemed strangely relaxed for such a nervous creature. Whether or not the rabbit with the gray spot intended to, Alechi caught it staring at him. When they arrived once more at the edge of the forest, Jerald set the rabbit down next to a tree and it took a few leaps before it stopped and stared back at them for a few moments.

"Go on," Alechi urged it, shooing it away with a hand gesture he could not hope for it to understand. It turned and retreated deep into the forest.

Jerald arched his back in a long, pop-filled stretch. "One last thing to do now. Replace the traps." Though daylight was drawing thin in the west, they baited and replaced the traps in the same place they had found them. They still carried their hunting tools in case anything revealed itself but nothing did. Night fell, day followed and the father and son duo were praised the next morning for their successful hunt. Each of the other hunting groups only managed to bring back a single stag for their whole day.

After Alechi and Jerald had finished their morning duties of gathering firewood, the day was theirs for leisure. Jerald took the wood to Calius' guardhouse and spent the day there with the guards talking about things that were never important enough to remember, but plenty of tea was had. Alechi decided to pass by and eavesdrop just long enough to hear his father boast, "I may have the strength of a bull, but I would not have been able to bring in *three* stags if it wasn't for Alechi's eyes! He was spotting the tips of their antlers while I was still looking for a head. He'll be a great hunter one day, I guarantee it!"

Calius then offered a toast, "To the future master hunter of Lagdin, Alechi!" The amount of laughter and shouting combined with the toast was excessive.

I'm not sure that's only tea, Alechi thought, turning to leave.

Alechi decided to spend the day in the village center with his friends. Though he should have been exhausted from the day before, he was as energetic as a grasshopper. Like many of his friends, and all of the young boys in the village, Alechi aspired to be a soldier that would defend Lagdin's borders in its time of need. As such, he and his friends often claimed fallen branches and pot lids from their mothers' kitchens as sword and shield to fight with one another.

Each of them made sure not to strike to harm or anything of the sort as they knew any injuries they left on another would be repaid to them tenfold by the shaman. Their miniature battles consisted mostly of flailing it around at their opponent in a mockery of fencing.

During such fights, some of their other friends who cared little for physical contact would cheer them on. One such friend was Eliya. She was easily the most beautiful of the girls in the group, at least in the eyes of Alechi, but few would contest the claim. When it came to the sparring between Alechi and March, his first and finest friend, she would sometimes play along as well. Sometimes as a damsel in distress, other times as a witch with a powerful wand that the two of them would put aside their differences to fight. She always won. Alechi and March considered it flattery.

Other days, however, the whole crowd of children would join in simple games such as Wolf and Sheep. On those days, time slipped through their fingertips like water on ice.

"Alechi!" One of his friends called out from across the market grounds, mildly disturbing the traveling traders looking for business from prospective young men.

"March!" Alechi cried back to his friend.

"Thou hast disgraced me and my family! I challenge thee to a fight to the death!" March declared with exaggerated pride.

"And I..." Alechi paused for dramatic flair, "Accept." His eyes became serious as though he were about to engage in a fight. But the moment they charged at each other, pot lids in one hand and short sticks in the other, their faces lit up with bright smiles as they exhausted all the energy they could to best their opponent. Their fights were more structured than those between some of Alechi and March's other friends. They enjoyed the dramatization of battle and did so with nothing more than fun in mind. Victories were traded, not earned, as, for the sake of their fantasy, the person who would win would always be the hero, the one who initiated the duel. One day March would challenge, and another Alechi would issue the fight.

Their fight lasted for many hours as they ran around the market area jumping on some of the terrain but always being sure to stay moving for both warmth and as a way to dodge the threatening "blade" of their friend. Throughout the whole fight, though she knew today's victor would be March, Eliya could be heard cheering for Alechi.

But, at last, it was over when March feigned a strike and managed to redirect the stick to his friend's chest. "Arrgh!" Alechi cried, dramatizing the blow dealt to him. "I am slain." He was not. "Thou hast earned thoust... honor... back... blegh." And with the last word he held the stick under his armpit, closed his eyes, stuck his tongue out and tossed his head to the side. He stayed like that for a few moments then shivered himself back awake and started laughing. March helped him up off the ground. But the theatrics did not cease at the end of the battle, for though Alechi was supposedly dead, he said, "Well fought, my friend!"

"And thee as well!" March responded.

With enough daylight left, the pair, with the reluctant permission of some of the guards, ventured to the outskirts of the surrounding woods. There they fought what they imagined to be giant actusfies much like the wolves that the shaman had frequently warned them about. They struck the trees while making all sorts of shouts and battle cries.

"I went hunting with my father yesterday," Alechi boasted, returning to his more regular mode of speech. "And he told me I did great!" The boys continued to swing the sticks at the base of the trees. Alechi continued with his boast, "I bet if I used that dagger he gave me, I could slay an evil spirit." He delivered a blow so powerful to the tree trunk that the stick snapped in two, sending a piece soaring into the wood.

"No you couldn't!" March disputed.

"Yeah, I could!"

"You lost today, remember?" he reminded Alechi, "If anyone could do it, I could. We both know I'm the better fighter anyway."

"I lost on purpose and you know it! I've always had the better sword arm."

"You wouldn't even see the spirit coming at you!"

"Yeah I would! My dad even knows, I have the eyes of an eagle!"

Their arguing continued with simple "Yes, I coulds" and "No, you couldn'ts" for what felt like endless ages to guards watching them. The guards finally stepped in when the sun met the deep horizon of the seemingly endless forest. Alechi and March were hurried back into the village and sent to their homes so that their mothers could not only scold them but so that they could eat with their families.

The guards pitied the bold, naive claims that both Alechi and March made while on the border of the forest. They had worked tirelessly to train for battle against the creatures and would not wish it on their worst enemy. But the boys craved nothing more than the glory they thought it would earn them.

When Alechi returned home covered in dirt and sweating from exerting himself the whole day, his mother met him at the door to scold him for being late. "Alechi!" she said to him, "Where have you been? I couldn't find you in the market earlier!" Then she noticed the pot lid, "My lid! I should have known you had it." She groaned at how dirty it had gotten, but then let out a deep sigh. "Did you at least have fun?" She asked, wiping off the dirt with her sleeve and picking at splinters in the pot lid. When she was satisfied with her work, she set it on the aromatic stew to keep things warm while they waited for Alechi's father.

"Of course! Though March said there's no way I could handle myself against an evil spirit even after I did amazing in the woods yesterday!"

"Alechi," his mother's tone grew serious, "you know that he's right."

"But I'm great at fighting!"

"But you are also still young. Your father was the one keeping *both* of you safe. And everyone knows I already don't like it just being the two of you out there. You know the rules, but do you remember why they are in place?"

Alechi tried not to roll his eyes. "To keep us safe."

"Exactly," she said. She bent down slightly with a rag in hand to wipe some dirt from Alechi's face she missed before. Under normal circumstances, he would have protested. But he was defeated and did not care enough in the privacy of their home. "Now, could you go get your father? I think he is still at the guard house."

"I, actually, am not," Jerald corrected as he stepped through the door.

"Just in time!" the mother exclaimed. "I hope you are not full of tea."

"I very well might be!" Jerald rhymed while slapping his stomach.

"And ease up on him, Ezri. He's still just a kid. Let him think what he wants. My head was filled with the same silly dreams when I was his age."

As they sent Alechi to fetch his siblings, Ezri and Jerald went to the side and had a brief dispute in quiet whispers. "But what if he goes out at night? He needs to know that he can't do that, especially if he goes alone."

"He is not going to get past the guards. Don't worry, they have eyes everywhere. And if you keep telling him that he can't then he will only insist that he can, then eventually he will."

"Fine, I'll 'ease up'. I just hope you are right."

Alechi returned, shepherding Beth and Casey toward the table and carrying Dailyn on his back. The family sat down at their low wooden table near the hearth and enjoyed a nice warm meal of vegetable stew with one of the rabbits from yesterday's hunt mixed in for a bit of meat.

3

The First Taste

During the dark winter night, Alechi had been restless. He could not fall asleep, he could not tell if he was too hot or too cold, but he knew he wasn't sick. At the forefront of his mind was his own ability to stand against the spirits.

Alechi was confident in his abilities to best an actusfie of any kind. He looked around the bedroom. Both parents still slept, and his siblings snored within the shadows, so he slipped out from beneath the covers of the low mat.

He crept over to the hunting chest using nothing but his tip toes. The biggest concern he had when he opened the chest was the creak of the unoiled, old metal hinge. *Creeeek.* Alechi winced at the noise and glanced to his family. After seeing nothing more than a dream's shuffle from his mother, he considered himself lucky they were still asleep.

Knowing what he was about to do, he decided to find a way to arm himself at the least. Using the dim light of the coals in the hearth to search through the chest with one arm, keeping the lid suspended and unmoving with the other, he found the dagger he used when he went hunting with his father. There were plenty more suitable and versatile weapons, but a dagger was all he knew how to use. He set the lid down slowly using his thumb to silence the landing of the lid on the body of the chest. The house was still asleep.

Alechi crawled to the door and took a deep breath as he prepared himself for the cold he was about to face. He felt some of the cool air coming in from the base of the door and knew that he would have to be quick about opening and shutting it. He stood up, placed a hand on the door and snuck out, closing the door softly behind him and watching to be sure his family remained as they were.

The night air was cool and crisp. It bit at his chapped hands and the wind did not move. The moon was full. Up above, not even a single star in the entire night sky was blocked by clouds, so he could see clearer still. Using the night's lights he strapped the dagger securely to his belt and walked heel to toe to the eastern gate. Even from afar, Alechi could see the bobbing torches used by the night sentries strolling around the closed gate. Larger fires, placed evenly atop Lagdin's walls, illuminated much of the remaining area.

Though Alechi was drawn as a fly to flame by the gates' torches, he knew he had to avoid them to make his escape. The well-lit walls left him unsure about how he could escape the safety of the village to challenge what he thought he could defeat. At all times a guard would stroll the ramparts above the gate making sure nothing was out of the ordinary, and two were posted at the side of each gate on ground level on the inside. The gates had long since been shut for the night, which only presented another challenge; even if he managed to slip by or distract the guards, he knew he could not open that gate himself. Not even Calius could move that gate on his own.

Alechi stepped from shadow to shadow through the village, eyeing the guards carefully from around the corner of the houses. He was looking for any semblance of a pattern in where they watched and walked. At length, he found one weakness in their pattern, a blind spot of theirs. He found a ladder up to the rampart some distance to the left of the gate and started climbing the moment the guard walking above the gate turned his back. The ladder itself was cold and somewhat icy, and he almost slipped a couple of times scrambling his way to the top.

He peered out over the ramparts into the dark forest. The dense, wild tree canopy blackened the entire area beneath. The sea of darkness within the forest was the only place he knew he could find an actusfie and prove to the others he could handle it. He felt in the back of his mind as he stood on the rampart a pull back to the village. A call not to make that leap into darkness. The shaman had always been very clear that no one should ever face an actusfie. Especially alone. *He only says that because he wants us to depend on him. He thinks we're weak. He thinks I'm weak. When I defeat an actusfie, then the shaman won't be needed in the village. Then people will treat me like an adult. I'll show everyone just how strong I am.* Those thoughts were all Alechi could do to reason his action, and though something in his heart told him he was wrong, he ignored it.

He vaulted over the rampart, plunging into the darkness beyond Lagdin's walls, and had no way to return until morning. So he was stuck out there, unless he wanted to be caught by the guards now. But it seemed a waste to turn back so soon. His landing was a little louder than he expected, even on the soft dirt beneath him, giving the guard above a moment of pause before swiftly ignoring the single thump as part of his imagination.

Alechi's eyes had adjusted to the dim light beneath the bright star-lit sky, but once he stepped underneath the trees he felt blind. The entire area was pitch black and he felt his way with his hands, pushing himself off trees and stumbling over rocks deep into the silent forest. An oddly quiet forest. No owls hooted, no insects chirped, and the ground was clear of all creatures that crawled or slithered in the dark. It was as silent as a blade of grass. If he wanted to, though he was determined otherwise, he could still see the light from the torches through some of the branches. They served as a beacon for him to follow and return home. And he thought about it for one last moment. About turning back home. About admitting his mistake. Then about the humiliation of a guard bringing him before the shaman. And it was then that his childish pride turned him to the forest and pressed him forward through the dark.

Each moment he spent in the dark forest, a fear grew inside of him. When his foot fell on a twig, snapping it, he became all the more aware of what he could not perceive. He ventured deeper and deeper with still nothing to challenge him but a few loose stones. The cold kept gnawing at his skin and he was poorly dressed for a full winter night in the dark, but he only thought about that as his bones froze underneath his skin. He placed his back against one of the thick trees and rubbed his hands and let out an airy breath to keep his fingers warm at the very least. He shook himself a little bit to warm the rest of his body, then pressed on.

Eventually, Alechi saw some light on the glade ahead of him. Letting out a heavy sigh of relief, he thought to himself, *A place I can see again.* He stepped into the glade and at the center was a stone where he could sit and gather his surroundings. The night sky cast a dim, cold white upon the glade where he sat and revealed the beauty of the various colorful flowers that were beneath his feet. He took a moment to rest here despite the thought that he may be vulnerable to the actusfies that lurked within the trees. How little he knew.

For the first time, he saw something move. Out of the tree line came a brown rabbit. The rabbit was rather large in size and approached him with very little sense of fear. It hopped around Alechi for a few moments and rubbed its nose on his leg. When it did so, he recognized the same light gray spot on its left leg. It was the rabbit he set free. It then swiftly turned away and made its way to the tree line he had come from, back toward the village. Before it entered the tree line, however, it looked to Alechi as if it was beckoning him to follow. He stared for a moment but then turned away and resumed his attempts at warming himself up. The rabbit repeated its process but to no avail; Alechi did not want to go home, not yet at least. One last time, the brown rabbit nuzzled his leg and urged him to follow, this time only taking a few hops from his leg instead of going all the way to the tree line. Alechi stood up at last and the rabbit hopped once more toward the tree line, but he did not follow.

"Leave me alone, will you?" Alechi said to the rabbit, feeling a little crazy as he did so. "There's something I have to do."

The beady, black eyes of the rabbit stared back, pitch black wells of pity and sorrow. Alechi saw, but did not let it move him. The rabbit retreated to the tree line in silence on the western side, back toward the village but stopped there and watched over Alechi.

A sudden surge of wind cut through the still air much to the surprise of Alechi. The chill settled deeper into him, deeper than the marrow within his bones. He paced around the stone to remove the cold, but it seemed to have grasped his soul. He ignored the cold, steeling himself to go further into the forest. Each step he took eastward, the rabbit would hop once toward him. Alechi would never leave the rabbit's sight.

He was bothered by the rabbit's stare as he moved through the woods. The silence of the night was only broken by Alechi's own breath and step until the wind cut through the trees again. The wind did not overwhelm him as it did before; in fact, the wind felt warm somehow. He followed the warmth upwind, drawing him as a horse draws a cart, and it only got warmer until he found a cave he had somehow never stumbled across before. It had been nearly an hour since he started wandering toward the soothing, yet unnatural source of warmth. New clouds above began blocking light from the night sky.

Then lightning struck and a thunderous boom soon followed. The rain started to pour down, so he rushed into the cave.

Inside his new shelter, he discovered it deeper than it had seemed from the outside. The water from the rain cascaded down the cave's overhanging edge and flowed down deeper into the cave. His eyes strained in the dark to follow the water, it was fascinating, but he would wait for the sudden storm to stop.

Then he heard a huff. And another. A bear stomped lazily toward the shelter, its unmistakable, dominating silhouette blacking out everything else in the forest. Alechi had no choice but to retreat deeper into the cave. With each backward step into the depths, he clung to the wall, keeping an eye on the bear.

The air warmed. As he was dragging his hand against the wall to steady himself, he felt a gap. The warmest the air had been. It was almost hot. He looked into the gap and saw a faint blue glow at the end before it turned. The bear grew louder as it approached. He went toward the glow.

He followed the thin gap, barely able to squeeze himself through, and came upon a shallow reservoir of clear water that seemed to flicker with blue flames. The bear couldn't follow him here, he knew that.

Comfortably warm and seemingly safe, as stranded as he was, he lay down by the water and its hypnotizing flames. Just before he was about to fall asleep, something in the water caught his eye, but when he blinked it was gone. He was unsure of what it was. Unsettled, he retreated toward the gap again.

You shouldn't do that, a voice told him. *There's still a bear back there.*

He stopped. Another shadow flickered beside his in the room. Unsure if it was his own, he turned wildly, searching for its source but found nothing. He tried replicating it, wondering if it was a trick of his mind. "Hello?" he whispered.

Hello.

"An echo?" he asked the cave, but when it did not respond again, he ruled out that possibility. *I have to get out of here*, he thought.

You would be ill-advised to do that. The bear is still out there. The voice repeated.

He agreed silently with the voice, thinking it was only him. A strange shadow appeared beside his on the walls again, fading before Alechi could guess at what could cast such a shape. Alechi felt his heartbeat quicken.

Oh, there's no need to be afraid.

He looked again at his surroundings and saw they remained stable, he felt sure he was the only one in the room.

You certainly are.

He stared back into the water.

Left.

He gaze shifted to the left and he saw something glimmering at the bottom of the water. *Is that a chalice?*

You should grab it.

He moved toward it but the water's flames flared higher as he approached.

Go!

He drew the dagger and tested the flames by sticking the tip in then feeling for any residual heat. He felt none. He returned the dagger to its sheath.

See? It won't harm you.

He waded into the water and pulled the chalice out of the depths and suddenly felt parched. *Why wasn't I thirsty before?*

Does it matter? You are thirsty now. So drink.

He sank the chalice, gold and gem encrusted, into the water and tried a sip before gulping down multiple cups.

Isn't that better?

But Alechi only continued to feel thirsty, but he returned to the shore of the reservoir.

I wonder if that bear is gone now. You should hide the chalice first, it will only get in the way and you can come back for it later. But where should I put it? You know, you could bury it with your dagger somewhere on the shore, no sense in getting wet again. Besides, if someone else finds their way here, you wouldn't want them taking your new treasure would you? Keep it here, far from everyone else, they may try to take it from you.

The water he drank now seemed to be filling his mind with a haze. It had tasted strange, but its warmth was pleasant, and it did not reek of the spirits the merchants sometimes brought with them to sell to the adults. He found a soft spot and used the dagger to dig a hole, placed the chalice in it, then covered it, smoothing the dirt over it.

Now you can safely check for the bear.

He squeezed his way through the gap again and poked his head out when he got to the main cave. Looking out, the stars were visible again and the bear was nowhere to be seen, but the rabbit was waiting at the cave's entrance.

You can go.

Alechi finished emerging from the gap and walked out the cave quietly in case anything but that rabbit was nearby. He sensed nothing else.

When he arrived at the mouth of the cave, it was the closest he had been to the rabbit since the glade. The rabbit looked at him with sorrow, not anger, and tried to once again comfort him and guide him slowly back through the woods. With each hop the rabbit took toward the village it looked back to Alechi. But he ignored it. He still wanted to face an actusfie. Straining his eyes to search, his eyes met the bright red glow of an actusfie's. *There!*

What are you waiting for? Charge at them before they get scared away.

With a ferocious battle cry, Alechi ran full sprint toward the eyes he could see. In his recklessness, he stumbled on a root a few feet from the first set of eyes. He could see the actusfie somewhat more clearly now. It took the form of a wolf, just like the ones he saw yesterday before taking the wood to Calius' guardhouse. Hauntingly slow, it began to grow. It continued to grow until it was over four times the size on all four legs as Alechi was on his two. He realized his mistake. The wolf made itself seem small and weak before revealing its strength. A common predatorial tactic.

He looked into the glaring eyes of the wolf as it let loose a deep growl. Another wolf approached from behind him and it grew as well. Then another. They kept coming until seven shadowy mountains surrounded him. He stood up. Although he was daunted by the size of the wolves, he took the dagger in hand and drew a deep breath, preparing himself to strike again. Letting loose another cry, he charged at the wolf that was closest to him but was quickly pushed to the ground by another wolf pouncing on his back.

The wolves were too strong for him. "If only I could just fight one of them," Alechi said aloud as his voice began to waver. "I don't want to die." He started repeating the phrase as the rest of wolves grew nearer. Their snarls silencing him when their mouths reached his ears. The wolf he had targeted loomed over him and opened its jaws wide.

Alechi braced himself for death, closing his eyes and accepting his defeat. But before the jaws would have snapped shut, he heard the wolves whimper like scolded puppies. The pressure on his back was released, but he was still surrounded. The rabbit was now so close that when he lifted his face his nose was inches away from its back. Using the opportunity given to him, he stood up again and readied himself to strike. But the wolves backed away slowly until they at last turned and fled like shadows before the dawn into the forest.

"Why do you have to ruin everything?" he asked the rabbit. Alechi's pride was in shambles. Night was beginning to fade. In the far east, the sun was rising. He had been out the whole night. Worse, he had lost his way back. "You just want me to go home don't you?"

The rabbit stared back as an answer. It took two hops in the direction of the village and waited for Alechi to follow. This time, he obeyed. A shallow mist began to settle in the forest as the moisture from the rain condensed above the ground. The rabbit led him carefully through the trees and checked to make sure he was there after every hop. The sun shimmered on the fresh, frosting dew and scattered itself between the leaves of the trees above. Under the brightening sky, Alechi stumbled much less. Birds began to chirp, and the woods came alive. Each footfall left a crunch on the frost. As he drew closer to the village, however, he felt warmer. Truly warmer. Feverish.

Despite feeling ill, he continued to press on toward the village. With each step he felt worse. *Maybe you should sit and rest.*

"No, I have to keep going," he said, leaning against a tree for support. He was almost home, he knew it.

But clearly you are sick, surely you must rest.

While Alechi leaned against the tree, the rabbit waited for him. It showed no sense of urgency. Despite how cold it may have felt, it remained still and watchful. Comfortingly calm. Alechi moved forward again and the rabbit began to lead again.

My parents are probably awake by now, he thought looking at the light from the sunrise cast his long shadow ahead of him. No longer was it just a light from beyond the horizon, he could see clearly now the waking sun. *I hope they aren't too worried.*

In the near distance, he heard the crack of splitting wood. Most of the families were already preparing the day's wood if not finishing up. He stumbled toward the sound. Through the cracks in the tree line, he saw the wooden barrier of Lagdin. *Home.* Although he stood now less than half a mile from his village, he felt weaker than ever and rested against another tree.

Weren't you going to kill an evil spirit? You can't go back, yet! You've returned with nothing.

"I have the cup!" He looked to his empty hands. "Wait..." he trailed off into despair. "No I don't."

You should keep trying for those evil spirits, it is more impressive to return with the heads of one of those than a cup anyways. The head would bring you fame and that cup, well at this point, it is just a cup. They would wonder why you stayed out the whole night for a cup, but if you returned with a head they would understand wouldn't they?

He moved forward once more and broke the tree line. The moment he did, however, he felt his weakest. Guards spotted him when they heard the thud of his collapse. The rabbit stopped and moved closer to Alechi and sat while the others approached to retrieve him.

4

Passing

When he finally woke up, he was lying between the fires of the hearth and his mother. Jerald was out fetching the day's wood alone as he had in most of Alechi's life and his siblings were tending to other morning duties, or at the very least pretending to. Ezri was still half asleep when her son woke up, but once she noticed, she picked him up and embraced him tenderly. "Thank the spirits you are awake," she said.

That's an interesting choice of words.

"You slept the entirety of yesterday and we thought we almost lost you!" Alechi could hear his mother fighting back her tears.

"I'm fine, Mom," he said after she released him, "really." Though he tried to affirm his safety and sanity, the tone of his voice hinted that he was still in a deep pain, even if he did not fully realize it.

"Are you sure?" Ezri asked, refusing to hide her worry. She cocked her head to the side, and let out a breath of relief as she settled into a more comfortable sitting position. She shared a slight smile. Somehow.

"Yes," he tried to affirm again. "I am."

"Don't push yourself too hard, okay?" she said. "If you ever need a single moment of rest, just come running, walking, crawling, or calling out to me. I promise I'll be there for you."

"I... will," Alechi said, forcing a soft smile to reciprocate hers.

"And please don't go out in the woods alone like that again." Ezri's smile faded slightly. Alechi had seen her angry, this was not it. But the stare she pointed at Alechi warned him she was serious.

"I... won't. Aren't you mad?"

"A little frustrated sure. I mean are you *crazy?* You could have *died!*" She sighed, calming herself. She wanted to yell, but could not bring herself to do it. "But you aren't hurt are you? I'm just glad you are home, safe and sound. I can't say I didn't see this coming. But just what were you doing out there, young man?" Alechi had earned much worse of a treatment than the gentle questioning she gave.

"I... just wanted to go to my hideout and see if I could last the night. And you're sure you're not mad?"

"No, I'm not mad." She smiled softly, ruffling his hair and accepting the lie. Her eyes reflected a thankfulness for Alechi's seemingly childish desires. "But never do that again."

"Thank you, mom," he said, returning the hug he received earlier much to the surprise of his mother. She was shocked for a moment and held her arms up while Alechi's wrapped tightly around her, then she lowered her arms and comforted him and ran her fingers through his hair, gently now, as she had done when he was much, much younger.

"Always and forever, Alechi," she affirmed him, "I will love you always and forever."

"I'm sorry I didn't listen," Alechi whispered.

"Always and forever," answered again.

"I'm sorry I worried you."

"Always and forever."

"I was scared."

"Always and forever."

They continued holding each other for a while.

Well that's enough of that.

Alechi then embarrassedly let go of his mother. His mother was equally as shocked as when he had grabbed as to when he let go, but she released him just as quick. Having seen her own brothers' temperamental love for their mother, Ezri understood she could not control Alechi's.

Alechi tried to stand up, thinking he was truly fine but his vision quickly went dark, his head heavy, and limbs weak. He had forgotten the hunger gnawing at his stomach and the thirst that comes with sleeping for a whole day. He fell back down and put his hand to his head.

His mother came and removed his hand from his head and placed her own in its stead. "I know you just got up, but you have to take it slow. I'll get you something to eat and drink."

He spent the rest of the day mostly resting but stepped in to help his mother whenever he felt he was able. Around mid-day, the shaman stopped by the house asking to speak with Alechi, but he said he was too tired to talk about anything. Despite the appearance of the shaman's stoic gaze, he suspected more was happening than just a child sneaking out to their hideout at night.

Later, though Alechi normally hated tea, when his father finally returned home he shared some with him and found it to be very relaxing. His mind would be clear and he could focus on the people in front of him. He soon discovered his mind would wander to strange places it had never endeavored to consider before, particularly when he was alone.

That night he went to sleep at a decent hour, yet when his father woke up for morning duties he was still sleeping like a cat on a summer day despite the biting cold of winter. When Alechi finally woke up, it was well past noon. Considering all of his other duties had already been attended to by his father, he sought his friends. The shaman stopped by early in the morning but, because Alechi was still sleeping, was once more dismissed for another day.

When he inevitably found March, there was quite the reunion. As always, March's hugs were suffocating.

"Please March," Alechi said, "I can barely breathe."

March finally released him and asked, "How are you feeling?"

"Good as new!" Alechi replied, "Though I'm not sure much changed." He examined himself and gripped his bicep to test its strength as he flexed what he deemed to be muscles.

Casey, finished with his own morning chores, wandered into the town center and noticed Alechi. He ran over and tugged Alechi's sleeve. "Can we play?"

"Not right now, I must duel my nemesis!" He smiled to March.

"Come on!" Casey begged.

"No," Alechi repeated.

"Please?" Casey asked again. He continued to tug and beg Alechi.

"Come on, Alechi," March said, growing tired of the incessant begging. "We can duel another time. Let's just play with him."

Casey grinned wide. "What are we gonna play?"

"How about..." Alechi said, entertaining a few ideas before settling...

Of course! You should play...

"Wolf and Sheep?"

Casey nodded excessively. He went to gather the other children for the game.

The smaller kids and a few of Alechi's friends lined up at one end of an imaginary rectangle within the village center, its boundaries as loosely defined as the shape of water. Alechi and March were elected to be the wolves for the first game and stood in the center of the play area. "Ready?" Alechi shouted, eyes narrowing as he focused on his brother. "Go!" There was a mass scramble as everyone tried to run to the other side. The goal was simple: survive. If tagged, the sheep would join the wolves. The last person standing would win. The children scattered every which way as they fled to the other side in hopes of making it to the next round.

Casey had eluded Alechi on this first run, but having tagged a few of the other children, there were five wolves ready to collect their sheep. The little brother giggled gleefully, glad he managed to survive, as he waited for the next round. Then Alechi shouted again and the next round began.

Alechi was determined to get his little brother this time. *You can't have your little brother be faster than you, can you?* the thought came to him. *Don't let him get away.*

Casey tried to run straight across in a playful attempt to pass right between the arms of his brother as they had done countless times before. Alechi would always humor him and let him through as though he could not catch him. But on that day, it was a mistake. His older brother charged right at him and tackled him to the dirt.

Time seemed to stop as thoughts raced through Alechi's mind. *Now is your chance. For what? To show him what a real wolf is like. But this is just a game. A game you didn't want to play. You just wanted to duel your friend but then he wouldn't leave you alone. He is my little brother. So? He is also your problem now. If you show him what a wolf is like, he'll never ask to play again. But now he's on my team. If you remember the wolves from last night, did they seem likely to bring you into their pack? No! So then why should he join yours? It's just a game. Is it? All he does is annoy you, now you have your chance to your revenge. Besides… aren't your duels more fun when you make them real? Are they not more entertaining to everyone? Are they not more thrilling? Why shouldn't this game of yours be the same? I suppose you're right. Where's the fun in knowing how it ends? Go wild! Be ferocious! A real wolf. I won't. It's all fake. Then make it real.*

And time resumed. He had made his decision, though he hardly remembered how. He shifted his weight and put his knee on Casey's chest, imitating the wolf that had held him down. He growled, formed his hands into claws and began swiping at his little brother.

Casey had been laughing moments before, but when the knee pressed into his chest, he struggled to breathe. He tried to push back against his older brother but his attempts were futile. He was too small to make a difference.

He's even fighting back! Don't you find this more fun? No. Just remember he asked you to play this game; this is on him, not you.

Alechi continued to make swing after swing and soon enough, his little brother was crying.

March, who had been distracted by the game, noticed what his friend was doing. He ran over and pushed Alechi off Casey. "Alechi! What are you doing?" Other children began to gather around Casey, trying to soothe him of the pain. March, though horrified himself, was the only one brave enough to stand near Alechi. The others dared not even look.

"I don't know," he replied after examining his fingernails. He saw traces of blood and only realized then that he had broken skin. There was no reason he could find that would constitute him going that far. Yet he had.

A guard, who had been more focused on the shops than a children's game, noticed the commotion and helped Casey back to his house while another guard asked the children what happened. Before the fingers of the other children could find him, he ran.

The shaman stood by, watching with only his sideways gaze. He understood clearly after what occurred what Alechi was facing but did not intervene for Alechi's sake. It was well enough known that should the shaman follow, it was a severe case. Should the others find out what he now knew of Alechi, the boy would be outcast.

Alechi ran away to a place he figured only he and March knew. Hidden near the tree line outside the village was a particular tree with roots that formed a cave. Though it was actually well-known to almost everyone in the village, only the pair of boys used it frequently as a hideout of sorts.

Finally, all alone.

The rabbit from the day before appeared at the entrance to the small cave. It stood still and its heart was moving at a slow, steady pace from what Alechi could tell. Its breath lulling like leaves in a light summer breeze. Then it took a few short hops closer to Alechi's side. Just then, Alechi began to cry. The guilt had been gnawing at him for long enough. He covered his eyes, hiding his tears from the rabbit.

Very mature, crying you know, and in front of this... thing no less. I hope you are proud of yourself.

"Just leave me alone," Alechi complained through the tears. "Go away!"

Oh but don't you see? We are one now. You should be grateful. Now get up. We have more important things to do than sitting here crying like a child.

Alechi felt compelled to listen to the voice, after all it would not stop nagging him until he did listen. He began to lift himself up but the rabbit hopped on his chest.

"Get off me!" he told the rabbit. But the rabbit was persistent and stayed on. The rabbit felt heavier than he remembered and its weight pushed him to the ground again. The rabbit then relaxed itself and its head rested on Alechi's heart.

They never listen, do- Yet the voice was cut off when the rabbit licked Alechi.

Stay.

The rabbit nuzzled Alechi's arms, encouraging him to hold onto the rabbit. He wrapped his arms gently around the rabbit and the tears from before resumed with a greater intensity. Yet, for a reason unbeknownst to him, he felt comforted and warm despite the cold of a late fall evening. The warmth felt as gentle and homely as a low hearth.

The sun began to set and the rabbit wrenched itself free of Alechi's grip. It went back to the entrance of the root system and waited for Alechi to get back up. He heard his name being called by his family and he thought he heard March's voice. He left the root system and the rabbit guided him, only a few steps ahead, all the way back to the gate, but it did not go through the gate. The guards spotted him and called out to those searching for him that he returned.

"Alechi!" his father said, Casey in tow. His grip was as firm as his tone.

When Alechi wiped the tears from his eyes, his father's expression softened. Jerald opened his mouth to speak, but was cut off by another bout of sobs from Alechi.

"I'm sorry, Casey," he said, as his voice strained to find its way past the lump in his throat. "I'm sorry I got so angry and hurt you. I'm sorry-" yet he could not finish his apology. He was surprised to find his little brother's arms wrapped tightly around his waist, as high up as he could grab. The little boy's arms were wrapped tightly in clean strips of cloth and the bleeding had already stopped, but Alechi took it as a sign of the extent to which he had gone and his tears built up again. He crouched to be more level with his brother and returned the hug. After a few moments Casey, finally separated, but Alechi was unsure if he was ready to let go of his little brother.

The father rolled his broad shoulders back and asked simply, "Are we all family again?" The two boys nodded. "That's good enough for me then. Come, we still have to get you cleaned up before supper." Jerald pushed Casey lightly toward home. "And Alechi?" His voice drew grave.

The boy could not meet his father's gaze, so Jerald lowered himself slightly to his.

"Double wood duty tomorrow." Alechi heard some sorrow in his father's voice, stern and stoic as it was. "It'll give you time to clear that head of yours. You know you're not supposed to hurt others. Especially not those who look up to you. Especially those you ought to protect."

Alechi nodded.

"Good."

When the group returned home, Ezri had already prepared a tub of water for washing. Alechi went first, rinsed his hands, splashed some water on his face, and wiped it all on the rag that lay beside the basin. He felt awake at last and for a few moments, he felt he had a clear mind.

The year began to pass, and by the eve of the next winter, Alechi had forgotten what it was like to have a mind free of whatever haze seemed to afflict him. He had forgotten how he felt with the rabbit and how he felt when he cleaned himself. His vices seemed to grow as his aggression to the other children increased and he would slack on his duties. Unfortunately, no one but the shaman said or tried to do anything about it. The shaman attempted once a month, so as to not draw attention, to help the boy. He would visit the family for a regular, friendly check-in, yet seek Alechi. But each time the shaman came by, Alechi would find an excuse to leave. The village seemed to expect such behavior from him considering his age; though they would remind him of expectations, they were not concerned when those were left unmet. The villagers of Lagdin were all too familiar with the rebellions of every growing child.

He seemed to spend more time alone. Alechi was hardly ever in his home or at any of the hideouts known to March, and distance gathered between them. March still held out for his friend, and sought him at every opportunity. And though Alechi knew March would make him better, that his family would make him better, somehow, he began to favor isolation.

In his time alone, Alechi would wander back to the cave and soon memorized the route as he navigated the forest. There he found his thoughts rationalizing his actions, reinforcing them as good. There he continued to taste the burning water, finding it sweeter by the day, yet somehow just as dull. It only strengthened his more dangerous thoughts.

On more than one occasion, his parents had reprimanded him for being so dismissive of his duties by merely holding him to them for the next day, after which he would neglect them again. His habits became a mystery as did his identity. He leaned heavily into his actions induced by thoughts that would have never occurred to him.

"I'm sure I did the same when I was his age," his father said on one occasion.

Alechi felt empty. Unable to remedy it himself, alongside the pangs of repeated isolation, the boy discovered a new attraction toward the girl who had typically played his princess in duels, Eliya. In every case, she too was one of Alechi's better friends. She had spent recent months helping her mother care for the newborn in their family, though she was really only concerned with doting on her new baby brother who she considered the most adorable thing in the village. That bar was considerably low, but nonetheless likely true for the whole world in her mind as well.

Her duties to her family and Alechi's sudden inward disappearance brought a new form of anxiety to the forefront of his mind. *What should I even say to her? Isn't that easy? You are friends, are you not? She will surely follow you no matter what. But I haven't spoken to her in months, does she even want to see me? Well you want her, don't you? I want my friends back. So you do want her. Well then take her to the cave.*

You love adventuring, do you not? So she must be the same as you, if you are friends, of course. It is quite a quiet, peculiar place, she would love it there... don't you think? And you know it is private...

As he thought of Eliya, he made his way to her home and knocked on her door. She was the one to answer.

"Alechi?" she said, as confused as she was happy to see her friend.

Alechi began awkwardly scratching the back of his head, "How are you today?" He tried to chuckle.

"I'm well," she said, closing the door behind her. "I'm just glad you didn't wake Fraien, I only just got him to go to sleep for his nap."

"If that's the case, do you want to come with me?"

She looked back to the door. "I don't know if I can. What if he wakes up?"

"He'll be fine, your parents will be able to take care of him," Alechi said, the ease of manipulation was almost frightening to himself. *You need to do it otherwise she'll never come.* "If he just went to sleep, we have plenty of time."

"I suppose..."

"Come on, I wanna take you somewhere fun?"

"Despite your and March's attempts, I know your hideouts, I don't really have ti-"

"This is a place even he doesn't know about."

"Really? What's there?"

"That will be a surprise. You have to come with me first."

She cracked the door open and looked over her shoulder inside. Seeing only her little brother breathing quietly asleep, she carefully closed it. "Lead the way," she said in an eager whisper.

He grabbed her wrist. The winter dusk was settling in, so they would have to sneak past the guards too. Though for all their stealth, and their success in sneaking around the guards, March had spotted them making use of a gap in the guards' poorly managed patrol pattern. He decided to follow, though he had not been as fortunate in his stealth. Calius was on duty, and instead of calling March back, he too decided to follow, bringing another guard with him.

The pair of children managed their way through the darkening forest, Alechi demonstrating his newfound knowledge of the area by warning of every dip in the earth or hidden rock or root. Eliya began to grow concerned over the distance travelled. The hideouts the boys had used in the past had never been this far from the village. "Can we go back," she asked, searching her surroundings for any threats.

"Why?"

"It's getting really dark, we shouldn't be out here," she said, making an attempt to wrest herself free from his grip. He felt the resistance and loosened his grip only to grasp her hand.

"Better now?"

"Alechi, come on."

"Relax, I've done this at least a hundred times. We are almost there." The cave came into view through a pair of trees and he helped her navigate over the fallen trunks and the steeper ground that preceded the cave.

The pair walked to the cave mouth. It was pitch black inside. Alechi began to step inside the cave, but Eliya held her ground. She refused to be moved from her place. The darkness made her sick, but the fear of what was inside surged new strength to her limbs as she ripped her hand from Alechi's.

"It's too dark," she said, massaging her hands for warmth and to relax them from the grip that had pained them.

"Eliya," Alechi said with a smirk, "that's part of the fun, isn't it?" He stepped back out the cave and forced a kiss. Then he craved more, he grabbed both her arms and pulled her into the dark cave, forced her against a wall and went for another kiss. But she was fighting back.

"Help!" she cried out, hopeless that her plea could be heard. "Alechi, stop! Help!" She was pushing against Alechi and turning her head. "Help." The strength was fading from her voice. "Help..." She was crying now and could no longer fight back.

Now you know she wants it, she's done fighting. No. Yes. No, I can't. Yes, you will.

Yet before a decision could be reached or another kiss planted, a voice cried out from atop the hill, "Eliya! Alechi! What are you doing to her?" It was March. He sprinted down and tackled his friend, freeing Eliya.

She felt relieved for a moment, then remembered the danger of Alechi, and now questioned even March's presence. She wondered what he intended as well, what he was doing at the hideout he supposedly didn't know about. Her mind spun into a confused tapestry of questions. But she found her wits again and ran as fast as she could back to where she remembered the village to be.

Now just March and Alechi remained in the cave. "March, what is wrong with you? You just ruined my chance with Eliya!"

"Your chance for what?"

Yet instead of an answer, Alechi wrestled himself out from under March and threw him to the side, concussing him for a moment. He looked outside the cave and could no longer see Eliya anywhere nearby, so he returned to March. Lifting him by his shirt, Alechi began to unleash a flurry of punches. March defended himself as best as he could and managed to land a punch into Alechi's gut. The enraged boy barely took notice of it. As another blow was ready to be delivered, Alechi's wrist was caught by a large, leather-gloved hand.

"Clever hiding here," the new voice said, clearly a guard. He threw Alechi to the ground. Alechi was in pain for a moment but soon realized he was properly awake. "Care to explain, Alechi, why we found Eliya wandering alone in the dark, crying? Ehrvan is with her now." He recognized the voice at last as belonging to Calius.

"Look, Alechi," Calius began, pausing as he was unsure of how to continue. "Everyone has been worried about you, you've changed so much. Your father won't stop talking about you, he's worried most of all but wants you to go to him. He doesn't want to pressure you into talking about what's wrong because he feels like he will just get the mixed answers he got when you collapsed in front of the village all that time ago. This, however, I cannot let slide. I have to tell the shaman about this, though I'm sure he already knows you've changed. This is beyond a line that any of us could have expected. This isn't just you being a boy your age. If I wasn't here to stop you, who knows what you would have done?"

You would have been satisfied.

"I don't know," Alechi said, not knowing if he was talking to himself or the guard. Calius grabbed Alechi's shoulder strongly at first then loosened the grip when he sensed no resistance. He helped March, who was struggling through a few fits of coughing while he regained his breath, stand, and the trio returned to the village.

When they reached the gates, Calius sent March directly home. Yet, before he left, March said to Alechi, "I'm sorry for tackling you, I just-"

"There's no need for you to apologize, March," Calius said. "You did the right thing. Alechi, on the other hand," he tightened the grip on the boy's shoulder again, "may have somethings he needs to say."

"Thank you," he mumbled. The grip tightened even more. "And I'm sorry."

"You are forgiven," March said, nobility rising in his voice. "Though I do hope you will never do that again."

"He won't," Calius answered. "Now go. Get cleaned up and get to sleep. I'll handle Alechi." March obeyed. Then Calius guided Alechi to the center of the village to meet with the shaman despite the late hour.

5

Recognition

The fire was lit, and smoke billowed out the chimney of the shaman's house. Calius knocked on the shaman's door and a voice called out from inside, welcoming them to let themselves through the door. The shaman was entertaining some of the traders with a meal and listening to their stories of dangers on the road. It was a clamorous environment that was full of laughter and joy, but the moment Calius stepped through the door with Alechi, the shaman's face drew grim and the room was deafeningly quiet.

"Thank you for escorting him here Calius," the shaman said, recovering from his initial reaction. He placed his hand on Alechi's shoulder, "I know it is easy for some to get lost in the dark and wander off." He gave Calius a subtle nod to dismiss him, and Calius left the home to wait outside.

"I'm sorry my new friends," the shaman said, "I had forgotten I made an appointment to meet with Alechi here."

We didn't have an appointment.

"We didn't-" Alechi began.

"We were going to discuss some things in a private matter related to which guardhouse he would be placed in," the shaman interrupted. He raised his eyebrows to signal for Alechi to follow along.

"I am nearing that age after all."

The shaman relaxed a little bit, "So if you could all go to your rooms upstairs and give us a little bit of privacy near the fire, it would be greatly appreciated."

The traders, already wearing from their travels, agreed and bid the shaman a good night. Just like that, the room was empty and nearly silent with the exception of cackling flames and the winds of the night sky.

He seems to lie easily to others, why wouldn't he lie to you? The thought seeped into his mind, making Alechi cautious of every word that would soon come out of the shaman's mouth.

"Alechi, I assume you know why I've been meaning to talk to you for some time?"

"I..." Alechi started, but he did not feel like he had the strength to finish.

"I'll take that as a 'yes'," the shaman said. He was keeping his voice relatively quiet and low, but it was hard and stern: a direct contrast to his mother's. "I would ask why you didn't come forward yourself, but I imagine that thing inside you has had a larger role in that than even you ever thought it could have."

There was no NEED to come forward. Alechi continued to hesitate, unsure of why he felt so defiant.

"I have a good guess of when this started," the shaman said. "Your actions do not reflect who you were, nor who I know you to be, and these changes..." the shaman trailed off for a moment.

You are an adult now! Nothing is strange at all about- the voice was becoming more distinct from Alechi's own thoughts.

"Quiet!" the shaman said, his words instilled a silence not only in the air but within the boy's mind and soul. "Now, Alechi, where was I... yes, these changes are too sudden-"

"How did you do that?" Alechi asked, interjecting yet breathing slowly and calmly for the first time in what felt like ages to him. "How did you know what I was thinking? Can you hear my thoughts?" Though even Alechi's voice made it clear he was uncertain they were his own.

"No. I cannot hear *it*," the shaman said with a careful enunciation. "But I've been around long enough to know when something is nagging at you." The shaman chuckled briefly to himself. "And I especially know when that something is not me.

"You are not the first to deal with something as severe as this, Alechi. There are people who can help you, especially if it is found early."

"So can you do something? Can you make it stop?"

The shaman looked regretfully at his own hands, "Unfortunately, at this point, no."

Alechi looked betrayed and stood up suddenly with an urge to run. "Then why?" His voice was breaking as he spoke. "Why am I here?"

"Truly enough, it was my fault, Alechi," the shaman said. "I should have pressed harder to speak with you sooner, before the actusfie had reached your heart." He placed his hand over his own chest.

"Actusfie? Do you mean the ones from the stories you told us as kids?"

"They were no mere stories, Alechi. The actusfie is dangerous. It is changing you, trying to isolate you. It wants you dead so that it can roam free. And I'm afraid one has latched itself to you in such a manner that I can no longer remove it. So—"

"Then why am I here? Answer me," Alechi was getting angrier by the moment. He knew that what the shaman said was true, yet every word stung more painfully than the last. The words each seemed to destroy more of Alechi's naive world than the last: that, in fact, the shaman and his parents could not do everything. "If you can't help me, then why am I *here?*"

"Because, Alechi, you crossed a line," the shaman said. "And while *I* may not be able to get it out of you, *you* can."

"I... can't."

"You *won't.*"

"No... I *can't.*"

"Alechi, listen, just for a moment. These actusfies are difficult to conquer and at times may feel entirely impossible, but if you fail to even try to fight it, it will tear you apart from the inside out. I can tell it already has been doing so. Your idea of yourself will completely change and with it your personality and actions. It is okay to grow up a little bit, it is not okay to lose who you are in the process."

"I can't fight it. I don't even know where it is. Is it not just a part of who I am now?"

"That is absolutely not true. Alechi, remember this, you'll never be able to start fighting it if you keep believing you can't fight it," the shaman said. He moved his hand from his chest and placed it on Alechi's shoulder. "I want you to trust me on this."

Warm, silent tears trickled down Alechi's face. His heart sank deep. The guilt and pain he felt was too overwhelming for him to even fully process so though he made no noise, every emotion he felt was clearly on display. "How?" he asked finally.

"If part of a potato is rotten, what do you do?"

"Cut out the rotten part?"

"And what happens if you don't cut out the rot?"

"The whole potato rots and it spreads to the other potatoes?"

"Exactly," the shaman said. "And what if a wolf is caught in a trap, what does it do?"

"Bites free?" Alechi's tears were beginning to slow.

"Yes. And what happens if the wolf doesn't free itself?"

"We come and kill it," that was the one thing Alechi was sure of. "Where are you going with this?"

"That actusfie inside you started out as nothing more than a little bit of rot on a single potato, now it seems like it has affected the whole crop. Now it also has you trapped in your own thoughts. It limits what you think you can do so that you will never do what you can."

Alechi moved back cautiously, "You want to cut it out of me?"

"No," the shaman said bluntly. "I cannot do that. It is far too dangerous for you. If we had caught this earlier I would have been able to say a simple spell that would have poisoned it and strengthened you in the name of Serinth and we would be done here, but now you have a larger task ahead of you. The point of cutting out the rotten part is to separate it from the good part, the point of biting free is to separate from the trap before it gets the trapped killed. What needs to happen now is separation. And only you can do that now."

"If I knew how to do that it'd be done already!" Alechi nearly shouted but caught himself. "Do you even do anything? You're just talking in circles!"

"Though I myself may not be able to help you, and trust me I wish I could, it is your journey to take. But I will give you what help I can. You have to destroy it at its source, get rid of the problem before it completely destroys you: as rot does a potato and a trap a wolf.

"You must make a journey to Som Catre. There they can help you separate you from it, and you must go quickly."

"Are you coming with me?"

"No, I must stay here, the village will continue to need protection, especially as the winter solstice approaches-"

"I'm going to miss the solstice?"

"You will." The shaman offered a soft smile. "But trust me, you will not be alone."

"I know... it will be inside me..."

"That actusfie will not be your only companion."

"Then who *is* coming with me?"

"That I do not know, but I do know that those with good hearts, as I know you are, are never left alone," the shaman gripped Alechi's shoulder and shook it, as if to instill courage.

"But I don't have a good heart," Alechi protested, brushing the shaman's arm away. "I don't even know what I was getting myself into tonight. I was going to hurt another friend... I was going to hurt Eliya..."

"That guilt is your friend, that shame is your enemy."

"What?"

"It is proof that you have a good heart when you feel guilt, and I can tell your guilt is genuine. Trust me, I've seen some others fake it. That shame, however, is what the actusfie wants for you, it wants you to feel defeated. It wants you to make your actions your identity. The actusfie will always lead you to shame and self-indulgence. If you don't indulge it, it will begin to separate from you, and you will be once more who you are."

"Then who am I?"

"You knew once, you just need to remember. I cannot answer that question for you. But for now, let's go over what you do feel guilty for," the shaman sat back, ready to listen. He looked Alechi in the eye as he leaned back into his chair, welcoming him to speak.

Alechi spoke out of what felt like necessity, "I've hurt my friends. My brother." He looked to the shaman for some response and was given a simple nod. "I've wasted so many days sleeping. I've put so much extra work on my father. I've ignored my parents, I've told them I hated them, I've lied to them, I've lied to everyone." Alechi stopped for a breath, realizing how relieving it was to get all of this off his chest. "I went out into the woods alone and got myself into this mess, I didn't come forward, and worst of all is that I never even tried to do anything about it. I was scared..." Alechi trailed off.

"Though I myself cannot pardon you of your wrong doings, you must ask for forgiveness from them first, and it will be given. I can, however, give you some advice. Fear, my friend, is the first of many foes we must conquer in our lives," the shaman shared, weighing each word as if a single misplaced syllable could cause the sentence to plummet in a set of scales. "You will be afraid, it will be difficult moving forward, but you must do it."

"And if I can't?"

The shaman smiled at Alechi's pessimism. "It is never a matter of ability, Alechi. If you do not believe in yourself, then believe in those who believe in you. If you do that, you *can* do anything." He gave Alechi another reassuring pat on the shoulder then stepped over to the door and knocked to let Calius know he could come back inside. "Calius, make sure Alechi gets home and, since I know you will anyway, give Jerald a 'Hello' for me."

"Gladly," Calius said.

"But then they'll know I got in trouble again," Alechi complained.

"Then tell them what happened... all of it," the shaman said.

"And no offense, kid, but you getting in trouble is not news at this point," Calius said matter-of-factly.

"Yeah..." Alechi resigned.

The shaman gave Calius a hard look, disapproving of the undoing that just occurred.

"Sorry, kid," Calius said, regretting the words he had spoken. "Let's get you home."

The walk was not long, but it felt to Alechi as terribly long as he imagined the trip to Som Catre. Calius was content to walk quietly with Alechi. The pair walked side by side and somberly as they walked toward the darker, sleeping parts of the village. Torches illuminated the area near the gates and the shaman's house but left a valley of darkness for the homes between.

The shaman doesn't believe in you. He doesn't trust you to even go home by yourself. You won't be able to stop, the voice, which was now differentiated in a strange, minute way, finally resumed once they were away from the light.

Alechi wanted to ignore the voice but it got him thinking, so he broke the silence with Calius, "Why couldn't I stop myself?" Though it sounded as if he was speaking to himself, he looked to Calius for an answer.

Calius was silent until he realized he needed to answer when he looked down and saw Alechi's begging eyes. "But you did, didn't you?"

"What are you talking about? You said it yourself: if you weren't there, who knows what I would have done."

"I may have pulled you off at the last second, but I heard that screaming and it took quite a bit of time to track where it was coming from. He's lucky I followed him, but Alechi you too played a key role in his safety, though you yourself were also the perpetrator. If you had no control whatsoever, you would have been a lot farther along than where you were when I found you."

"But I didn't stop myself, I had multiple chances to slow down. To stop. But I didn't."

Calius stopped to think of a way to explain. "Just because you did not succeed in stopping does not mean you failed in it either."

"What?"

"I think that will make sense eventually!" Calius laughed to himself. "You'll understand soon enough, I hope."

And he's just an old fool, nothing he says will ever make sense because it is simply nonsensical.

A few moments later they arrived at Alechi's home. They knocked on the door and Jerald answered it. "You're back early, Alechi." He looked at the guard standing next to his son, "Calius, what did he do this time?"

"All I know is that I am supposed to say 'hello', so... hello."

"Alechi?"

"I'll explain but I want to talk to Mom as well."

"Fair enough," Jerald said. He gave a terse nod to Calius. "Thank you for bringing him back. Good night, Calius."

"Good night, Jerald." Calius nodded in his reply then returned to his patrol on the gates.

Jerald went to go wake Ezri, and the three of them sat on the far end of the house, away from the others who were sleeping. "Mom, Dad," Alechi started. "I'm sorry."

"What for?"

"Let him finish, Ezri," Jerald said. Then he whispered into her ear, "He's finally talking to us, just let him do it."

You don't have to do this you know, you're just going to cry again... like a child!

Alechi hesitated as the thought stung his heart. He knew the words to be true, but it is because they were true that he had to continue. "I'm sorry, I've been lying to you," Alechi then explained the whole story of what he had done on that winter night last year, the actusfie that he now knew resided in him, what he had nearly done tonight to Eliya or rather what he did do to Eliya, and what he did to March. Once he started speaking, even if the spirit tried to break in to interrupt, Alechi refused to even notice its presence. His voice was strained as he spoke and he was fighting back tears the whole time, trying desperately not to break down. He was heartbroken and he was the one who had broken his own heart. In that brokenness, however, he was entirely honest with his parents about everything he felt over the last year. "I'm sorry," he repeated.

Jerald was silent for a moment. "I don't really know what to say. I mean of course I forgive you for lying about it."

Ezri agreed, "As do I. And I think I speak for both of us when I say we are sorry you ever went through this."

"You're not mad?"

His father responded, "Surprised for sure. It's a lot to take in." Jerald looked to his wife then back at Alechi, "We're happy you finally feel like you can be open with us. It must have been hard."

The pain of coming clean always cuts deep. It was clear that Alechi's parents felt for his pain, as if it was somehow their fault he ever fell into that trap. But there was love too. "I wish I could go back," Jerald said. "I really do. I wish I could have prevented any of this from ever happening. I wish I had noticed what it really was and acted sooner. I've failed you, Alechi, and I wish I never had."

"This isn't your fault, Dad," Alechi protested. "I was full of myself. I got myself into this mess."

"And we'll be there to help you get out of it," Ezri said, placing her hands on Alechi's.

"Thank you," Alechi said weakly. "Thank you." Alechi leaned in and hugged both of his parents in front of him and the trio stayed in each other's embrace for a good, long while.

When Alechi finally let go, Jerald asked, "If there is ever anything you need us to do for you, just ask and it will be done."

"There is one more thing and I don't know if you can help me with it."

"What is it?" Ezri asked.

Alechi explained the situation as he understood it in regard to how he now would have to travel to Som Catre to rid himself of the actusfie. "I know you can't come with me. I know you have to look after Beth, Casey and Dailyn. But I will take anything you are willing to give me."

Jerald thought carefully for a moment. He went over to the hunting chest and retrieved the very same dagger Alechi had used that night last winter and handed it to him. "It may not be much, but you can take this with you."

"Thank you, but won't you need this for your hunting?" Alechi asked, unsure.

"I guess this year is the year I team up with someone else," he laughed a little bit. "We'll just use theirs for now."

"And of course we are going to make sure you have enough food for the journey ahead, but don't let any of it go to waste," Ezri interjected, standing up to go prepare a sack.

"Thank you, mom," Alechi said. "But I don't leave until morning, so you can relax for a bit."

"It never hurts to be a little extra prepared," she said with a smile.

"For now, let's start with something simple," Jerald suggested, "Let's get you some sleep." Alechi was far from tired but he knew he would need the rest for the coming journey.

"Actually, Dad," Alechi said, "can you come help me with something?"

"What is it?"

"I need to apologize to a lot of people for sure, but I really need to apologize to Eliya."

"And you need me for that?"

"Well... you know her dad," Alechi said. "I just need you behind me."

"I can do that."

Alechi and his father walked over to Eliya's home and Alechi led the apology directly to Eliya and her father, "I'm sorry, Eliya. I'm sorry I betrayed you. Betrayed our friendship. Betrayed the trust. Betrayed my duties as a man. I'm sorry for hurting you, for treating you like... like nothing instead of a person, instead of as a friend." Then he directed his attention toward the father, "Sir, I am sorry I ever put your daughter in such a situation. And I'm sorry to bother you this late at night, but I needed to say it." Throughout the whole apology, Eliya stood behind the protective arm of her father, with her arms folded over her chest. She never turned her body toward him. Alechi looked at her again. "I hope we can be friends again."

Eliya's father looked at his daughter then spoke, "I appreciate the apology, young man, but what you did is going to be hard to forgive. I suggest you keep away from my daughter, or I don't think I can be as gracious next time. I'm sure your father back there understands."

"Of course, sir," Alechi said, quivering from more than just the cold. "I hope there will never even be a next time, for either of us."

"Only you can be in charge of your own actions," his father said. "It's good to see you are taking responsibility for them. In time, should my Eliya ever desire to be near you again, I expect you to treat her with respect and dignity. And to protect her as you would Beth or Dailyn."

"Of course, sir."

Eliya rushed deeper into the house and the father stayed a moment before giving Alechi another serious, deadly stare and closing the door in his face.

Alechi let out a sigh of relief that he had not just been beaten to a pulp as he expected. His father startled him however when he placed his hand on Alechi's shoulder, "You'll understand soon enough that though he may look scary on the outside, he's a generous enough man. I knew you could do it without me here too, you know."

"I know."

"Ready to head back, or do you need to make one more stop?"

"One more."

Jerald nodded approvingly, "Then we go to March's house."

When they arrived, Alechi knocked on the door and it burst open. Alechi was instantly tackled by March, and Alechi held his arms up to protect himself from what he expected was to come. Instead, the weight on his torso was relived and a hand offered. He took it. "There," March said, rubbing his still aching jaw. "Now we're even." The injured boy smiled back to his friend. "Nothing you do would ever make me unwilling to forgive you," he said. Then he cocked his head slightly. "You did come to apologize right?"

"Right. I'm sorry, March."

"Thou best be," he said. "Now, get some rest, and we shall meet again for a rematch!"

"Of course," Alechi said with a sad smile. He could not bring himself to tell him he was leaving.

6

Setting Out

Nothing was particularly unique about the morning that Alechi set out for his long journey. He was woken by his father at the time he should normally get up to help with other morning duties and he prepared himself for the journey ahead with what strength his tired body could muster.

Ezri was awake, too. "Here's the food I packed for you. It is not going to last you the whole way if you eat like you normally do, so use it sparingly."

"I understand, Mom. Thank you."

"And don't forget the dagger I gave you," Jerald said, handing it to him once more. Alechi saw little use for such a small blade.

"Thank you, Dad. I can't believe I almost left it."

"I expect you will return it to me when you come home though. No more sneaking out with it." His smile was hiding a pain known only to fathers.

"I got it," Alechi said, smiling back. "I promise I'll come back with it." Hope was building in his heart. The actusfie hated it.

Not if you get caught out in the woods or along the road. You are going to such a dangerous place and they are sending you there alone with just a knife. You remember how that went last time.

Crushed, the smile disappeared from Alechi's face, and his clammy grip tightened around the dagger. "Hey," his mother said softly. "Remember, you're never truly alone. I know the axuli are looking after you. They always have." She offered as much as a smile as she could manage. Sending a child away was never easy, and this was her first time.

But that line from his mother almost made him angry.

How could you have gotten into this mess if there was an... a thing like that looking out for you?

"Then why did this even happen?" Alechi choked, shaking as he fought back the beginnings of tears. "Why? Why was I alone then?"

"Honey," she said. "They were there. Probably making sure

things did not get any worse. They were helping in ways you may never even know." The thought was only somewhat comforting to Alechi, but it was enough for now.

They have not done anything. You would be dead if not for me. You were spared as those weaker spirits were held back not by one of those, but by one even stronger! You wanted a chance to kill those spirits, but you let them get away.

The actusfie's words continued to haunt his thoughts. It had crossed his mind before that the rabbit may have been an axuli but now he was unsure. The rabbit had *seemed* to protect him, but perhaps the actusfie was controlling the other spirits. Perhaps the rabbit was bait to keep them close. The debate continued in his mind as he tried to rationalize whether or not the rabbit had been the thing protecting him or if it was all a façade. He was pulled from his trance when his father placed a hand on his shoulder and said, "We should get moving."

Already on his way over, the shaman walked slowly but purposefully and caught them as they exited the house. From there he took over as Jerald left to go attend to his regular morning duties.

"Goodbye, Dad," Alechi said. "I love you."

"I love you, too, Alechi," Jerald said. "Come back safe."

"Come now," the shaman said. "I, too, have some supplies to offer."

Most people were attending to their regular morning duties, and for them it was a shock to see Alechi awake this early again. A few with keener eyes noticed that he was dressed not for a simple morning splitting firewood, but for a long journey with a pack on his back. He had donned a cloak and a warm coat fastened with belts. Though the sun was far from rising over the horizon, it forced a hazy blue to appear in the east that was enough for the villagers to see the strange set of circumstances. Made stranger, in the eyes of some, by the fact that he was walking with his mother and the shaman instead of his father. The shaman guided them to his home at the center and welcomed them both inside.

Once inside, Alechi was told to sit down, so he did, and his mother sat next to him. The shaman disappeared deeper into the home and returned shortly with an old iron sword and a small leather buckler that had both definitely been heavily worn in previous ages of combat. "Now, Alechi, I know you are used to playing with sticks and pot lids, but these are real and can hurt others. They are not the most refined tools but they will be enough, I hope, to fight whatever may come for you. Use them wisely. Carefully."

"Where did you get these?" Alechi asked.

"There are many like it, swords that are well worn from ages past and the shield is the same; however, this set is the last I have to give. It was my own from when I was young." Looking at the sword and buckler, the shaman aged from a rare grandfather to an impossible hundreds-years-old elder in Alechi's eyes.

"Old..." Alechi thought aloud. Catching himself staring at the shaman, he snapped out of it and asked, "Why is this the last set? What happened to the others?"

"Remember what I said, Alechi? You are not the first to encounter this problem. Now this set is yours. Unlike that dagger at your hip, I do not expect this to be returned to me. These are yours now and when you succeed..."

If you...

"Quiet," the shaman ordered as he had before. He stared at Alechi knowingly and continued, "*when* you succeed I ask that you keep them as a reminder of your victory."

"Thank you, sir."

"Well then, it is time for you to go. I think you have everything you could need. Don't be afraid to ask others for help either," the shaman encouraged him. "Other people and the axuli are more willing to help than you may think."

"Of course," Alechi stood up and began to make his way to the exit. His mother and the shaman followed him out.

They walked to the northern gate of the village, one Alechi himself had rarely gone through in all of his time in Lagdin. He felt he was about to step out of the village for the last time, waging in his heart a war between hope and despair.

The northern gate was far less occupied than the eastern or western in terms of villagers present in the morning. A pair of guards stationed above the gate were the only ones watching and were far more concerned with what was happening beyond the village walls than what was happening within.

"Alechi," the shaman said when they got to the gate, "there is something else you should know. Or rather something you should know by now that I don't think you do."

"What would that be?"

The shaman leaned in to whisper in his ear, "Whenever I tell that actusfie to be quiet, I'm not the one that exerts the power over it. That's you. You don't have to listen to it."

Alechi's face began to contort as the thought began, *That's not true in the slightest, he's the shaman, you're just a boy, of course he-*

"Quiet," the shaman ordered again. "Trust me on this, Alechi. You have more strength than you know. Remember *it is not* you, but it will try to tell you whatever it wants. Do not listen to it. It truly fears the axuli. Fears your strength. Anything that casts doubt on the axuli or your value is unlikely to be you."

"Okay."

His mother stepped in closer to Alechi and hugged him tight. The morning sky was turning a bright orange as the sun peeked over the eastern horizon. Then she held him at arm's length and asked, "Are you sure you don't need to say goodbye to your sisters? Your brother? March?"

He looked down almost regretfully for a moment before confirming, "I'll be back soon enough, right? No real reason to say goodbye." He forced a smile as his heart raced. The journey that lay ahead of him was not going to be easy, and he knew he would not be back soon enough; only never leaving would be soon enough for him. He wished he did not have to leave but knew that he must.

"Then I suppose you really are ready to go. I pray the axuli will keep you safe," his mother said.

"As do I," the shaman agreed with a nod. "And remember what I told you; you are stronger than you know."

"I know," Alechi said, annoyed with how hard the shaman was pushing that idea. Even if he knew it was the truth, hearing it so often made it feel like a lie.

He took his first step beyond the gate and the guards posted above looked with great curiosity at the solo foot traveler coming from their own village. They looked behind them and saw Ezri and the shaman waving him goodbye and just shook the confusion from their heads, thinking nothing more of the whole situation. Alechi stopped before the dense trees cast the trail into utter darkness and turned around, waving one last goodbye to his mother and to his home.

Looking forward, Alechi took a deep breath and stepped into the daunting tree line. Though day was still increasing the light above the trees, it had no effect on the road below. The wind was still. He stayed in the center, eyeing the trees for whatever he feared, whatever loomed in their shadows. He wanted desperately to turn back, afraid of everything he may soon encounter but the shaman's words echoed. *Fear is the first of many foes we must face.*

It is also frequently the last.

"Quiet," Alechi attempted.

Oh, so you think you are a shaman now.

Alechi furrowed his brow and narrowed his eyes, "Quiet," he forced again, through his gritted teeth.

The actusfie remained silent, and Alechi considered for a moment that it had worked; unfortunately, however, the words it left lingered in Alechi's mind. Clearly, he thought, the spirit was misleading him, as it always had, and was trying to scare him. Though he knew this, he still walked afraid of every rustle in the bushes and every snap of a twig. His heart was racing out of his chest even while he tried to control his breathing, but any attempt to soothe himself only made things worse. The road and forest were hardly haunting, yet fear held him.

"I can do this," he assured himself. "I just have to believe in those that know I can." He pondered what he said for a moment, then burst into frustration, "It still doesn't make sense!" A pair of nearby birds fled their branches. Alechi stopped walking just to kick some loose sticks and rocks on the road, lashing out as dust clouded up around him from the violent movement. Once he was out of sticks for his kicks, he scanned the area around him for any more, and seeing none that seemed worthy of his time to break, he finally resumed walking.

He flared his nose and bit his bottom lip hard while he walked, angry at the nonsense he deemed to be the shaman's advice. Maybe the actusfie was right, maybe no one believed in him, and maybe he did not have anyone he could believe in. Assuming that would have even worked. As he walked, he tried to keep his focus on the road ahead, but the terrors he imagined behind the trees demanded his attention more often than he could refuse. It was a well-trod path, but that offered Alechi no assurance of his safety. He knew that merchants often hired mercenaries due to the dangers of a road so far from Som Catre. The dirt was a sandy yellow that generated a cloud of dust with each pounding step that built up on Alechi's already well-worn sandals and pants. The coarse, rough dirt climbed up his pant legs, irritating the skin that it touched. "It just gets everywhere," he complained as he raised his leg to sweep his pants as clean as he could manage.

The wind picked up suddenly, almost knocking him back as the gust threw even more dirt higher up. All of the tree leaves shook, rustling as if being torn through by a violent storm and letting a few streaks of light scatter beneath the dense canopy. Some of the few older and weaker trees creaked at the will of the wind. Alechi shielded his eyes from the gale while doing his best to prevent himself from eating anymore dirt the wind threw at his face. Bits of dirt stung his arm and after what seemed like an eternity, the wind slowed and died down.

"What was that all about?"

Just another reason you should not be out here, it is unpredictable.

"I thought I told you to be *quiet*."

You know you could turn back now and-

"Quiet!" Alechi shouted again, interrupting the spirit. He knew he had to go forward, it was a journey he would have to take eventually; one he now knew he would rather have done sooner. Alechi breathed a sigh of relief and forgot whatever it was that had upset him. "It's working."

Oh, I wouldn't be too sure about that.

"Quiet, Quiet, Quiet!" Alechi fell to his knees, shutting his eyes and covering his ears as if the actusfie's voice was coming from outside him, though he knew it was not. He sat on his heels and begged, "Why won't you leave me alone?"

Well, I am a part of you, not apart from you. You and I are one, we are the same.

"No! Just shut up!"

The actusfie did not respond but whether that was its own compliance for its own nefarious purpose or because Alechi had seized control, the boy was unsure. Regardless, he relaxed and stood up again to continue walking.

Alechi dared to look off the road to see if he could spot anything interesting. Along the road were various colorful flowers and a few patches of grass that had survived many years with what little sunlight broke through during the winter and early spring as life burst through the forest. Though the flowers themselves were few and far between with many more of them being weeds that sustained themselves by draining the life of the forest they lived in, despite the grass yellowing and dying, Alechi still considered it beautiful.

The hours began to pass and his feet were soon sore. Most of the journey thus far had been along a steady, but shallow incline that gradually got rockier. Alechi looked along the winding road ahead and it was full of many rises and falls. At the end of what he could see, nothing more than a sliver ahead, he saw what seemed like the steepest slope yet to come. Most of the trees around him were thick and strong, deeply rooted in the earth, standing tall. One of them in particular had a pair of roots that made for a nice almost cradle to sit in and rest. Alechi made his way to the tree and sat at the base. He took out his waterskin and took a few sips from it. He felt the weight of the water, gauging it to be about half empty.

"I need to find a stream soon," Alechi said to himself. For him, speaking aloud was the only way to remember things nowadays, and he would rather remember such essential needs. The last thing he wanted was to run out when he was too far away to find any. "There should be one near here... March always knew where to find one."

Earlier that day when March woke up to cut wood on the southern side of town, he suspected nothing particularly strange about the day to come. His head and hands were wrapped in cloth bandages, but they did not seem to slow him down. He went with his father and the pair chopped plenty of wood before March went to check on the strawberries his family grew in front of their house and picked a few small ones for himself and placed some larger ones in a basket. He brought them to his mother to include in tonight's dinner.

"I'm going to head to the center. See if Alechi is there," March called back to his house as he walked away without waiting for confirmation that someone heard him. He wove through the houses and narrow streets before arriving at the center. Morning had long since passed when he finally arrived and saw some of his other friends beginning their play fights. The laughter and pants of physical exertion filled the air in the area. A pair slowed, then stopped once they saw him approach.

"March!" one of them cried out, "You're finally here! We were thinking of playing Wolf and Sheep. Which team?"

"Wolf. Is Alechi here yet?" March stood on his tiptoes and peered around the entire area looking for any sign of his friend.

The other boys hesitated and looked at each other before one spoke up again, "We haven't seen him all day."

"Well, *kind of*, anyway. It's because he's not here that we want to play... wolf... and sheep," the other said.

"What do you mean 'kind of'? What do you mean he's not here?"

"He went to the north side of the village with the shaman this morning, my parents saw it happen," the first said. "Everyone's been talking about it all morning."

"Yeah, because Alechi did not come back with the shaman," said the second. "He was packed with enough for a while it seems. I don't think he is coming back."

"No," March said staring at his friends, waiting for one of them to crack and reveal it was all some kind of joke. "No way." March stepped away from them and ran to the north side of the village to see if he could find Alechi.

"He probably got banished," the first shouted. "The shaman doesn't just send people away like that!"

March ran in disbelief of what he had heard and arrived at the north gate to find the road ahead empty. He felt a weight sink into his chest. He used all of his strength to shout at the top of his lungs, "Alechi!" The cry echoed faintly in the distance. Knowing now that Alechi was long gone, he ran back to the center with what felt like a thousand eyes watching him as he ran and knocked rapidly on the shaman's door.

The shaman did not open the door but rather a confused merchant. "Oh, good morning, March," a voice said from behind him. It was the shaman, who now ushered the merchant back inside with a list of apologies and took his place at the door. "Can I help you with something?"

"Where's Alechi?" March asked. So worried of the answer he feared, he added, "Did you banish him?"

"Where'd you hear that?"

"The others said they saw you walking with him to the north gate this morning and he didn't come back. What's going on?"

"... So he really did not tell you?" Then the shaman muttered to himself with a slight chuckle, "Even when he's gone he's making work for me."

"Tell me what?"

"I had to send him away on a quest of sorts. Though nothing as fantastical as the ones the two of you always imagined. He should be back eventually, though even I do not know how long it will take."

"Why?"

"That," the shaman said, "I am not at liberty to explain. He had his reasons, I just sent him along. He should be well prepared though." The shaman smiled. "Have a little bit of faith in him, and he'll be back before you know it."

"So he's not banished then?"

"Oh, no. Just occupied. Would you like to come inside and have some tea? I just finished my rounds. Your other option," the shaman turned, "it seems, is the game of Wolf and Sheep your friends are waiting to play with you."

"I don't want any tea, shaman."

"Well then off you go. Go! Have fun. For Alechi's sake."

March nodded then rejoined his friends to explain what had happened to Alechi not according to rumors but according to the shaman himself. Most of them were just surprised to hear that Alechi had not been banished despite everything he had already done and a few were just as relieved as March, though only a few. "Where's Eliya?" March wondered. He knew something had happened between his friends the night prior, but still was unsure of what.

"She's been inside all day," one of the friends spoke up. "Probably just looking after her brother."

"Probably... I'm going to go see if she's there."

"What about Wolf and Sheep?"

"Play without me!"

"But!" One of them cried out in an attempt to stop him but he was already too far away to even bother trying to strain his voice to reach him, so he sighed, "We were waiting for *you* to play..."

March arrived at Eliya's home and knocked twice and was greeted by a man that towered over him. "Is Eliya home? Can she come out to play with us?" March asked. "We're about to start Wolf and Sheep."

"Eliya," the man called softly toward the inside of the house, "would you like to go out with the others?" No sound was made but the man nodded then turned back to March. "'Fraid not, kid. She doesn't seem up to it. She has not been feeling well lately."

"Okay, do you think she'll be better by tomorrow?"

"It's hard to tell considering everything that happened."

"What happened?" He could remember only vague images from the night before and remembered even less about what happened before Alechi attacked him.

"It's not my place to say."

"I've been hearing that a lot lately... well, I'll come by tomorrow," March said, with sudden determination. "Get well soon, Eliya!" He called out to the inside of the house, just hoping she could hear him from wherever she hid.

March left the home but did not return to the center of the village, instead making his way to the north gate and sat underneath the archway. "Before I know it, huh?"

7

Descent

Alechi stood up and scanned the nearby area for water. He knew he was more likely to find some near the base of the hill than the peak. March and common sense had taught him as much. But the dense trees blocked out any hope of spotting any part of the brook, much less streams. He listened carefully, hoping to catch the sound of running water but he had no luck. The howling wind, rustling leaves, and singing birds drowned out any sound of water that he might have been able to hear. Alechi weighed his water again and decided he would risk waiting a while longer to search for water. He looked into the tree line to justify himself, *It's already risky enough being out here alone on the road...*

He started walking towards the hill ahead. As he drew near the hill, he saw a break in the canopy near the top, and it caused light to shimmer down through, illuminating his path, welcoming him to the struggle of the hill. *I guess this is another reason we don't get a lot of traders,* he thought, realizing just how dangerous it was to descend this steep of a hill on a cart. The descent would be reckless one way, and the ascent, nigh impossible. Though he had just rested, the hill proved to be even steeper than he imagined. His legs were tired and heavy, as if weights had been strapped around his ankles, but he continued to climb on, determined to see what the light above had to offer.

Soon enough, he reached the peak of the hill and saw clearly through the canopy for the first time since he left the village. An ocean of green stretched far and wide, far off in the distance he could see the beginnings of the mountain range but still saw no sign of the river. It was buried beneath the tree line. Had he been more observant, he would have noticed the dip in the treetops where the river lay. Suddenly, his mouth felt even more parched, reminding him of the gnawing thirst. He couldn't see too much ahead of him in terms of a path. The shining sun was setting on his left, casting an unsettling glow on the leafy sea beneath him. After spending so much time beneath the dark canopy, he feared what it would be like once any semblance of light had passed from the world. Alechi had nearly given up hope for finding signs of human life when he thought he saw a freshly rising pillar of smoke in the northeast. It was still a long way off but it was still a marker to follow.

You'll never make it before nightfall. You might never even make it.

"Even I know that," Alechi said aloud, trying to quiet the spirit with all of his will power, yet it did not change the fact he was still disheartened by the daunting distance that remained. His eyes were fixed on the distant smoke, wide with longing for his own home and a warm fire. The season neared Winter's coronation, and Alechi could feel it in his bones.

I never made you do anything. Your ruination is your own.

"Shut up," Alechi said angrily. "You're lying. You made me consider things I never would have considered before I met you."

Considering is different from acting.

"Shut up!" Alechi ordered again. He felt the guilt, the pain compound each time the actusfie spoke to him. He tried his best to resist its words but they stung deep like the thorns of a fresh rose. Every half-truth only increased Alechi's anger and despair.

With the fading sunlight, Alechi remembered he would need to find a place to stay for the night, and the top of the hill seemed like a good enough place. He only had a pair of blankets, one thick for the ground and another thin to keep him warm enough while he slept. He scanned the nearby area for a spot that seemed flat and found one he deemed sufficient on the side of the path. The day had passed as quick and silent as a leaf in a rapid. Making as best use as he could of the dusk light, he found as many leaves as he could from previous falls and piled them under his thick blanket as a faux cushion for his head.

"Never thought I would be preparing for bed before dusk faded," Alechi thought aloud. Though he normally stayed awake a few hours past nightfall, tonight he couldn't resist the call of rest. He had no idea if he could have found a better location to stop for the night. He lay himself down, but the moment his head hit the pile of leaves they proved to be useless. His head sunk to the ground.

You can't even get that right.

"Shut up," Alechi said, doing his best to ignore his discomfort. "If it means shutting you up, I'll sleep in a tree."

As you wish... the actusfie's voice trailed off menacingly but Alechi ignored it.

Alechi finally closed his eyes to rest and, despite the environment being harsh enough on him, fell into as deep of a sleep as he could manage. As he slept he had a dream. In the dream he saw a horned, towering, ethereal giant standing right in front of him and it raised its arm slowly. Then the giant, maintaining its slow movement, sent a fist the size of a house toward him. Alechi dreamt that he was unable to run from it, though he knew that he had plenty of time to do so. Before the ethereal beast could damage any part of Alechi's dreamworld, the fist took a sudden turn upward and drew the rest of the beast with it as it morphed into a winged, serpent-like figure that unlatched its jaw as if roaring or preparing to swallow whole. Though he could not hear any noise in the dream, he knew its roar was terrifying and in that terror he awoke. It was a call.

He sat up suddenly as he sweat, feeling as if a fire had been set beneath him. A pair of birds were chirping wildly above him, quite unusual for what he judged to be a little past midnight. All he really knew is that he did not see any signs of morning light and the moon was beyond his sight. Alechi did a quick check of his surroundings, but in the darkness he couldn't make out much more than shapes, which only further fueled the flames of his fearful nightmare. The birds above him continued to chirp, and Alechi did his best to ignore them. He knew he needed sleep for the upcoming journey. He did not want to be tired. He could not afford it. His exhaustion bested his caution, and he lay his head back down to sleep.

The dream resumed. Though this time it opened on a cloud of smoke. The smoke seemed to take the shape of some noble, kingly figure that bowed to something that Alechi could not see. At the top of the figure's head, the smoke faded into a fierce battle in the midst of a war. The battle expanded to envelop Alechi as well, forcing him to wake up. He looked around again, still hearing the birds chirping, but saw nothing in the darkness of the trees. Despite the fact he was terrified and annoyed at the unfortunate restlessness of the birds, his exhaustion dragged him once more into the darkness of sleep, silencing the whispering light of fading stars.

Alechi woke up a few minutes later without a dream he could remember but instead was disturbed by the birds that had descended from the branches above him and were chirping loudly in his ears.

The birds landed on him trying to peck him awake. It was too dark for him to tell what kind of birds they were, so he swung his arm to shoo them away. "I'm trying to sleep!" he told them angrily, "Can't you just let me do that?" He finally had a dreamless sleep, and the birds had robbed him of it. He forced his eyes shut in a desperate attempt to attain such sleep again. Then he heard the warning: a distant howl. Alechi shot up like steam fleeing a pot of boiling water.

You might want to get up in that tree... the actusfie's voice sounded sing-songy, as if it was toying with Alechi.

But Alechi stood petrified. The howl was answered by echoes of similar howls that edged closer as he stood still. He remembered the terror of the wolves eyes as they stood over him, threatening death. One of the birds pecked his feet, healing him from the fear-induced paralysis, then flew into the tree branch it was in originally. Alechi quickly slung his sack over his back and started climbing the tree, then stopped suddenly. He thought silently, suspicious of the birds that had annoyed him, "Isn't this what the actusfie wants?" Which, in fact, it did want, but not for the reason Alechi would think. After the briefest moment of contemplation, he concluded the birds must be controlled by the villainous spirit and that's why they wouldn't let him sleep either. He dropped down from the tree and started running down the hill as fast as he could, leaving his blanket and the chirping birds behind.

The howls grew more frequent as he ran blindly along any path he could manage. He knew his goal was downhill, there he could find water. *If I manage to cross it,* he thought, *I might be able to get away.*

Have you considered that maybe they could swim?

Alechi, distracted by the thought and vain attempts to track his pursuers in the dark, forgot to watch the ground in front of him. His foot caught a root and he took a hard fall, tumbling down the hill for a few rolls. Had he been playing with his friends, he would have just stayed down, but fear motivated him to move more. A sharp pain shot through his right leg and he stumbled to stand. He continued to move as fast as he could with his limp. He was breathing fast and his eyes were wide, searching for any sign of anything that could give him any more trouble than he was already experiencing. Then he heard a howl from directly behind him and quickened his pace once more. He winced in pain with each dragging step, the sound of his seething nearly drowning the rush of water ahead of him. *Water!* His mouth felt parched once he heard the water. Alechi looked hurriedly for any nearby sign of light. Surely, he thought, that if there was water, there was a break in the trees; unfortunately, however, he could not see any sign of such a break or of any moonlight. He continued to run as he searched. The water grew louder and louder as he got closer. Alechi's ears told him he must have been right on top of the water, it was not the loudest stream but it should have been right underneath him. As he stepped carefully forward, his first step sank into a shallow stream no deeper than his ankle and his other brought him to the other side of its bank.

Oh that will definitely stop a pack of wolves, the voice said, clearly sarcastic.

"It has to work," Alechi said, out of breath and only half-believing himself, "It'll work."

If you insist...

"It has to work now," Alechi reassured himself. He collapsed from exhaustion onto his palms and loose sticks and pebbles poked at his hands. He breathed hard and slowly. The howls continued in the darkness, sounding closer than ever before.

Suddenly, Alechi heard a rustle in the nearby bushes on his side of the stream bank. Alechi groaned, realizing that whatever was about to show itself to him he would have to face without a chance to run but the actusfie had a different plan.

You should run.

"I can't," Alechi said, rolling onto his back to relieve the pressure from his hands and knees.

You should definitely run if you want to live. No, I'm dead already... Only if you stay still. Quickly! Get up and-

The actusfie's voice was cut off when the creature in the bush revealed itself. It was the rabbit. Not any rabbit, but the very same one that had rescued Alechi before. It was here once again, though he could only make out the rough size of the creature. He knew it wasn't a wolf, but since he could not identify exactly what it was, he still cautiously crawled backward. The rabbit hopped over to the river bank standing between it and Alechi. A strong wind erupted out of nowhere, causing a rather significant break in the canopy to appear above the rabbit. The starlight illuminated the small stream and gave Alechi a clear view of the courageous rabbit. As always, the rabbit seemed calm to Alechi, ready to face anything. The rabbit remained still even while the wolves' howls grew louder and closer, echoing throughout the entirety of the wild forest. The pair of birds soon flew in as well and set themselves down on either side of the rabbit. Once the birds had settled themselves, the rabbit crossed the shallow stream with one grand leap.

The first few wolves tore through the bushes and low branches on the side opposite of Alechi, grinding and gnashing their teeth. The next wolves strolled slowly through, cautious and growling as they approached. Seven wolves in all showed themselves between the trees. Six crouched low as they threatened to pounce on the rabbit at any given moment. They snapped and barked, the starlight revealing bloodstained teeth with every sound. One wolf in particular did not do any of these, it stood tall and paced slowly and proudly in front of the other six, weaving through the trees in its way. It did not gnash its teeth, snap, or bark, but merely walked, maintaining a low, harsh growl. It dared not get any closer to the rabbit than it had to, tracing an invisible semicircle eight yards from the seemingly insignificant creature. The growls, barks, and snaps told him enough about the wolves. But the mere steps of the proud wolf terrorized Alechi's heart. The twigs and loose leaves on the ground shuffled with each powerful step as if blown away and broken by an intolerant wind. The wolf stopped its pacing and let out a loud, single howl that tore through the sound of the roaring wind, yet the wind continued to blow, refusing to be overcome. The howl silenced the gnashing wolves.

The rabbit made the first brave move as it hopped toward the wolves, laying itself humbly on its side. The pacing wolf approached, maintaining its deep growl as it walked. The low growl deepened for a moment before it stopped. Alechi could see the wolf more clearly now that it was standing near the light. It was larger and even more fearsome than he could have ever imagined. It had dark gray fur and its eyes were even darker. It bared its teeth as it stood over the seemingly helpless rabbit. Its teeth were the only ones unmarred by blood or stain. Its knife-length claws reflected what little light there was in the area as they tore through the long fur at the base of its feet.

The wolf raised its claw and placed it slowly onto the body of the rabbit. It waited a moment, pressing its claws deeper into the rabbit with every heartbeat of the rabbit. The rabbit winced in pain as blood began pooling at the tips of the claws but stayed still. Alechi could have sworn the rabbit turned its head to him. Even though he could not see it all clearly, Alechi felt the pain of the rabbit's gaze. It let out a pathetic yelp. He stood up weakly, leaning to one side so as to not put pressure on his injured leg. He reached slowly for the sword at his waist and for the buckler that sat atop his sack. As his hand touched the pommel of the sword, however, one of the birds promptly flew up and pecked his hand, reminding him that he could not truthfully fight the wolves. Alechi felt helpless as the wolf dragged its claw against the length of the rabbit before turning it over to repeat the torture again.

You can save it if that thing really means that much to you. Don't you remember? They did not let you sleep. They are against you. You should fight. But Alechi understood well-enough now that the birds were on his side—the rabbit's, not the actusfie's.

The actusfie tried to dismiss the rabbit as if it was not doing anything. The other bird then fluttered up and pecked at Alechi's head to break his focus away from the actusfie's thoughts. With that peck, Alechi fell nearly limp with fear, relaxed his arms and fell on his knees, one after the other, sitting on his heels as he surrendered any chance he had to fight. One of the wolves in the back leapt forward from one of the distant trees to make a run for the defenseless Alechi. It was smaller than the first one, but equally as terrifying if not more so. The smaller wolf was scarred and bore a thicker mane around its neck than the first and when it bared its teeth it bled. The wolf was stopped in its pursuit when the rabbit shifted its gaze away from Alechi and directly toward the wolf that dared to dart. The smaller wolf whined and retreated to its place hidden within the trees.

The bloody mud beneath the rabbit only continued to make its wounds sting more as the first wolf played with it for a few moments longer. Then, seemingly out of nowhere, the wolf lowered its head and opened its jaws wide and bit the rabbit's neck with lightning speed. A small, short whimper was heard then silence. The wind that had kept the light shining through the trees died down and no more light was visible to Alechi, even from within the rabbit's eyes. The wolf picked up the dead rabbit and carried the lifeless corpse back into the forest for the rest of its hunting party. Though Alechi could not see it, he heard the ferocious shredding of flesh combined with barks and growls. The wolves were fighting over that small rabbit and had forgotten, at least for now, about Alechi.

"Thank you," Alechi said, the words barely leaking out of his mouth as he tried his best to fight off the tears.

It didn't do it for you, you know. There are two more here just like it that are actually worth saving not- but another peck, this time just to the area above his heart, made the voice go silent.

I know I'm not worth- but he was cut off by a peck to his lips. The birds were oddly efficient and it almost seemed to Alechi like they enjoyed his pain. He stood once more and ran away, following the stream up as best as he could. He ran away from the horror he had just beheld, away from the birds that insisted on pecking him. His eyes were slow to readjust once more to being in the complete darkness of the forest and he continued to move as fast as he could, too afraid to even dare to look back. He hoped that while those things were distracted with the rabbit, he could find that village or some break in the trees where the stream hopefully got thicker, but it just seemed that the canopy got thicker.

I don't know where I'm going, Alechi thought wearily, lacking the energy to even force enough air through his mouth to speak. The birds understood the wordless plea as they followed him closely in the tree branches above. They left their branches and flew out and above the canopy to search for something. All they had done, in Alechi's mind, was scare him once more.

As he ran, the branches began to part and the stream got progressively wider. It was a gradual change but now that the trees were not as tightly bound over one another, he could start to see through to the sky above him. He felt himself walking uphill and though the water itself flowed softly at times he could feel a splash come from the stream. He was short on breath. He looked behind him and saw with what little light found him that nothing was following him. And he realized he ran the entire distance in silence. There was no sign or sound from the wolves. He sat at the base of a tree and checked himself for his supplies. The cool night was swift to remind him that he had left his blankets behind.

Well, would you look at that. You're lost in the middle of the forest without your blankets. But here's some good news! At least day is coming soon. You can walk safely in the light... can't you?

Sure enough, the actusfie was right. The entire night had passed by the time Alechi finally sat himself back down and now he could see the dark sky changing to a hazy morning gray. He barely had any sleep, and he knew he had to keep moving. It was only safe for him to travel during the day and he did not want to be caught by another pack of wolves in the night. He stood up and continued to follow the widening path along the side of the stream occasionally having to weave around trees that were on its bank.

He dragged his feet along, and by midday, when the sun had risen almost directly above the thin gap in the trees, he stopped again. He needed to refill his waterskin and cool his aching feet, so he stepped into the stream. The dirt lifted from his feet and was washed away with the rest of the stream. The water was nigh freezing, but Alechi was reminded just then of his childhood, of playing in the water by the village with his friends. The water reminded him of home... *Could the stream lead me home?* After staring silently and solemnly at the stream, something in him decided it was not yet time to turn around. He took off his shirt, hanging it on a nearby branch, and scooped water to wash himself, or at the very least his upper body, of as much dirt as he could find.

Alechi withdrew his feet from the water and hurriedly dried them to keep the water from freezing them off. He put on his shirt, picked up what baggage he had, then started walking upstream again.

The water started to widen more rapidly, speeding and rushing as it did. He was walking up an even steeper slope than before. His pace quickened as he hoped to soon find the village he had seen so long ago. He figured it had to be near water, but he still saw no sign of smoke in the breaks of the trees. It was nearing dusk once again. His heart began to sink deep into his chest, he could not bear the thought of another night out in the wilderness completely alone.

Though it started as a silent, distant din, he recognized the sound of crashing water. That sound gave him a spark of hope. It was unlikely the village was near a waterfall but it was certainly possible. In his pursuit of the sound's origin, he followed it until it drowned out any other sounds he may have heard.

Soon enough, just before night fell upon him entirely, he saw the waterfall with his own eyes. At its base, a large pool of water spread off into a multitude of streams. It was beautiful as the reds and oranges of the fading light reflected off the pool of water. It was the brightest area Alechi had seen since he left the village. While he still had light enough to see, he scoured the area for a place he could sleep and found a cave near the base of the waterfall. He cautiously tossed a few rocks into the cave to check for any bears or wolves that may be hiding in there. He had enough of those. Luckily, however, the cave had been empty for some time. Not even animal bones remained. It was a small enough cave that soon after entering its opening he was able to feel the back wall. It was cold and damp in there, but Alechi still thought it would be better than sleeping in the open. He tucked his arms into his shirt and settled himself against the back wall. The exhaustion that had begged him to rest ever since the night before took him to a swift, sudden sleep.

8

In Darkness

It *was* *still* *dark* when Alechi awoke in the cave. He wanted to sleep more, but his body would not let him. Leaving his gear in the cave, he stepped outside near the pool to see if he could guess the time, but he could only recognize the bright center star around which the whole night sky spun. Most other stars were veiled behind thin clouds.

The crashing waterfall was the only real noise he heard. Most of the nocturnal animals were essentially silent compared to the water. Even though it was night, he could still see better than he could during the day while he was under the dense canopy of trees. The moon's light reflected brightly off the pool of water even through the clouds.

Shouldn't you get moving soon? Now is not the time for you to be sitting still.

"I feel as if I've earned my rest here, so quiet," Alechi replied, annoyed. He continued to explore the areas he could see, but avoided the dark as best he could.

You haven't done anything to earn rest.

"I ran from wolves through the night."

And who's to say they are done chasing you?

Alechi believed the actusfie, he really had no reason to believe they were not still following him. And whether he wanted to admit it or not, he knew deep down that he recognized that wolf that ate the rabbit as the one that he first encountered last winter. The leader of that pack of seven. They had hunted him this far and could soon be nearby, but he heard no sign of them. "I just need a break."

How do you expect to save yourself while doing nothing? You must keep moving if you want to live. The actusfie's influence on Alechi's mind continued to strengthen, yet that made it even more distinct.

He was afraid. It was not necessarily a new sense of fear, but it was a fear that the actusfie could exploit. Just as the actusfie had used fear before to entice him toward the flames in the bear's cave, it replicated the terrorizing howl of what sounded like the distant proud wolf. The moment it did, Alechi was faster to react, refusing to stay frozen in fear for any longer than he heard the howl.

He quickly went back to his cave and retrieved what was there of his gear and started to move. Alechi did not know where the howl had come from, but he hoped it was not up river. The problem, he soon remembered, was not where the wolf he thought he heard was coming from, but where he could realistically go. He hated the idea of turning back for even a moment and losing the river again and he had no idea how wide the cliff face was and how far away he would have to track it. He saw no other way for him to go other than to climb up the waterfall.

Alechi was cautious of the craggy cliff. But it seemed to have plenty of holds, so he started climbing despite his aching body and tired mind. When he first started his climb, he lost his footing a few times while still near the bottom, only falling a few feet before being determined to get back up and climb lest he be devoured like the rabbit. Many of the rocks were slick with water and moss, but Alechi was fortunate enough to find deep enough holds that he could scale the whole cliff.

The night seemed to last for an eternity. *Is it the solstice already?* Looking above, he saw the brightest star was not yet centered in the sky above. It was close.

He climbed slowly, careful not to look down and behind him, but the wolves' howls haunted his mind. *The wolves could be right behind you.* He climbed faster and more careless. His walking sandals were a poor fit for climbing and struggled to grip on the slippery wall. Alechi's upper body strength had never been grand, not to his or to anyone's knowledge, but somehow each time his foot slipped he managed to hold on with his arms without even risking a fall. The gear on his back made the climb more difficult and even more treacherous should he fall as he did at the base. He placed one hand after the next, one foot after the other.

About halfway up the 30-foot cliff, he reached for a deep hold and once he placed his hand on it, he felt it gash and pulled it away from the wall fast. A razor-sharp rock hidden in the wall had opened his hand, forcing him to rely on his two feet and his one remaining arm. Clenching his fist to staunch the bleeding, he refused to cry— not out of strength, but out of fear of attracting wolves. He looked around the cliff face for any place he may be able to sit and saw a ledge a few feet from where he was on the wall. The adrenaline of fleeing the wolves and the imminent danger of falling if he moved allowed him to ignore the pings of pain in his palm. He winced whenever some of the dirt from the wall crept into his open wound, but was able to make it to the resting place on the wall, leaving a trail of bloody hand marks in his wake. The moment he sat down, he felt free to breathe again, only now realizing he had been holding his breath the whole way across. The wound stung, but at least now he had an opportunity to close it; he would have to wash it later as now the waterfall was too far away for him to reach. Alechi tore a strip from the base of his shirt, praying his mother would understand, and wound it around his hand.

From where he was, he could not see a clear way to climb as he had before. Now, it seemed, that he was farther up the wall, he had a clearer view of the path he followed last night. It seemed as treacherous as death. A miracle that he had survived running through the forest.

So you're dead either way. It's hopeless. Just jump down and make it swift.

"What? No... I... I have a chance, I think."

You think thinking will help you here? Your thoughts never matter. You know you cannot do it. Look at this cliff, you have bitten off more than you could chew. Just like that rabbit.

"No..." Alechi started, remembering the sacrifice the rabbit had made for him, "No I have to keep going. Just shut up."

You will die eventually, what reason is there to delay the inevitable?

"I said, 'Quiet!'"

No, you said, 'shut up,' and that is not very polite.

"Just leave me be, I need to focus."

Look, can you really climb that? Alechi looked hesitantly at the wall, *No, you cannot. You are going to die anyway. Whether you fall from this wall, die of starvation, cold, or by the very wolves still chasing you.* The actusfie once again echoed the sound of the wolves in Alechi's mind though no other creature could ever hear it. *You have a chance to choose your death, that is all there is to your life.*

Alechi stood up and looked over the edge he stood on, allowing his mind to go blank as his body leaned forward, but something reminded him of the pain of a fall and he leaned back into the wall as he shook himself from his trance.

He took a deep breath and did his best to remember everything he had been told before he left Lagdin. "Believe in those that believe in me. Trust that they know me better than I do. I can do this. I'm not..." he looked around and saw nothing near him, no birds, no rabbits and certainly no other people, "alone." Tears welled up in his eyes and his heart sank deep, "I *am* alone."

Yes, you are. No one is here to help you, no one is here to save you, hold you, and there never will be. This was a death sentence of your own doing. You sought the "challenge" out, you made the choices that led you here, abandoned and alone in the wild.

"I just want to go home..."

Then go. Just act like you are healed, no one else has to know.

"I can't go home..."

You cannot go forward, not when you are this lost. You should just fall off, no one will find you. No one will know.

"No one would know..." Alechi repeated mindlessly. Then his resolve shifted. He said with confidence, "My parents would miss me."

They will not miss you. With how much trouble you caused them, they might even be relieved.

"March would miss me," Alechi challenged, hesitant to contest the claim the actusfie made of his parents.

You beat him up, and he has completely moved on too. You were a terrible friend, he is better off without you.

"Eliya..."

Do not even think about her. You are the last person she wants to see.

"Beth, Casey, Dailyn..."

All you have ever done for them is terrify them, especially after what you did to Casey. You were not even close to them. They probably have not even noticed you are not in Lagdin!

"Then I really do have nothing," Alechi said, defeated. He accepted everything the actusfie told him. "But I don't want to die..."

Then what do you have to live for? Who haven't you pushed away?

The shaman's words came to Alechi in that moment and he remembered, "I have a good heart. The axuli are with me."

Are they? Do you see any magnificent spirits out here? They've abandoned you. You will never get to Som Catre. You will never succeed, you could not even scale this cliff!

Now Calius' words echoed in his mind, he repeated them aloud, defying the despair, "Just because you did not succeed in stopping does not mean you failed in it either."

That is just nonsense. The lack of success is the definition of failure, and that is all you are.

"Just because I have yet to succeed does not mean I've failed," Alechi said firmly. "Just because I have yet to succeed does not mean I've failed. Just because I have yet to succeed does not mean I've failed."

Oh great, now you are just speaking nons-

"Quiet!" Alechi's resolve was firm and the voice was banished for now. His hope was returning, "There are those who believe in me." He looked up the cliff and started climbing again, pushing through the pain of his wound. "I can succeed. I will succeed." He assured himself as he climbed. "There *are* people waiting for me, I just have to keep moving forward."

Soon enough, he was able to reach the top of the cliff and he looked back down triumphantly at what he had conquered. He had trouble remembering why he was so defeated, why he thought he was going to die, why he had to get to the top. While he overlooked the sea of trees from a clear view for the first time in what felt like ages, he was able to take a break and drink from the river flowing to the waterfall. The air where he stood was clean and crisp, so he took his opportunity to breathe for a few moments. The sun rose in a gray haze in the midst of the morning dew.

He sat overlooking how far he had come in awe of it all before realizing he truly had no idea where he was. He had completely lost the path to the next village, the path which ultimately led to Som Catre. And his only way forward that he could imagine would be along the river. The trees atop the cliff on which he sat were farther apart than the dense forest in which he was walking before and the light shimmered on the ground beneath the leaves. The sparse leaves allowed a healthy amount of sunlight to reach the patches of weak grass that grew by the base of each tree.

There were very few animals in the area, at least few that revealed themselves even to Alechi's sharp eyes. A few fish were swimming in the clear waters farther up the river, particularly in areas where the water was calmer.

Once Alechi had decided he was ready to move on, he set his

gear at the base of a tree and climbed up to peer through the branches near the top of the tree, hoping to spot any sign of a village or even a lone house anywhere.

Looking all the way around he saw a singular pillar of smoke billowing in the near distance. He knew it was the same pillar he had seen the night before and seeing it now to his left, he realized just how far east he had gone. How he had covered that much in a single night was truly amazing—a feat worthy of knighthood as March would have declared—but Alechi was too focused on the defeat of losing the trail that would likely have led straight to that pillar of smoke. It seemed like a reasonable distance away, but he had to hope that he had not climbed that cliff for naught. If he discovered the home was below a cliff of its own, he was unsure if he could climb again before properly bandaging his wound. The moment he started thinking about the pain in his palm, it started to sting unlike it had before. He clenched his hands together to put more pressure on the open wound in an attempt to alleviate the pain before finally carefully descending the tree.

It was time to move on. Alechi retrieved his bag and started walking in the general direction of where he had seen the smoke. The path was far clearer and luminous, and he was able to walk confidently on the uneven ground, blazing a new trail as he walked.

On occasion he started to see the wildlife, he spotted a pair of deer eating some fallen nuts between the trees while rabbits were hopping carelessly throughout the forest. Squirrels were scampering up and down trees and were the most cautious of Alechi's presence, fearing him to be a thief of their precious, hoarded food. Some curious animals made a cautious approach before dodging behind some trees to continue their watch; most, however, just continued about their normal business, scavenging for food, singing songs, or chasing the other animals around.

Alechi hoped deep down, though he may not have even realized it, that he wanted so desperately to be comforted by the creatures as he had by the rabbit from his village. Or pecked by some of the sparrows as he had the day before. He wanted some sign that the axuli were watching him. His confidence grew that the rabbit truly was an axuli and had wanted to help him.

And you let it die.

Alechi continued walking, doing his best to ignore the actusfie.

That thing's death was your fault. You watched in fear. You did nothing to help it. You just let it die, and for what? You are a coward not worth saving.

"Shut up," he started, but he couldn't find the strength in his heart to deny it. He had no way to rationalize why he was saved. He had no idea why he didn't do anything. He had no idea why he ran as the rabbit was devoured.

See? You know it is true. You aren't worth anything. Your family is doing fine without you. They managed for twelve years without you. What use do they have of someone as pathetic as you?

"Maybe you're right... maybe no one needs me."

They may miss you for a moment or two. Humans are sentimental after all, but after those seconds, they would move on with their lives. Some people from your village already assume you are dead and they are happily continuing their lives without you. They have all moved on from you.

Alechi's eyes dropped to the ground, halting in his tracks. His sack fell off his weakening shoulders. He could not bring himself to look forward any more than he could bring himself to pick up his sack. Already the sky was darkening. He loosened the scabbard from his belt, letting it fall, flung his shield forward, and fell onto his back onto the hard earth. He ached everywhere, only now noticing because he had stopped fully. Alechi did not want to keep going, he wanted his journey to already be over. He had left the trail behind and was uncertain of what river he was even following. Then, he let his head fall to its side and looked at the water flowing beside him. "Everyone moves on," he said with a weak voice.

Your death is expected.

"They know I'm going to die."

They are ready for it. Your death would not even be tragic, you cannot expect a tragedy.

"They may even be happier."

They are happier without you there.

Alechi couldn't move himself, he just lay there, staring longingly at the river that likely led home in some way. Night continued to settle in. He could feel himself falling into sleep as slow tears fell from his eyes down the short fall to the ground. He gave in and slept.

When he finally awoke, it was the dead of night, a sight he was unhappily familiar with. A time he associated with the wolves and all his shortcomings. Checking the stars, he knew it would be a long night. *It's the solstice.* He was reminded of his initial encounter with the actusfie, the way it snuck into his life, and how he let it in. He remembered how he beat his brother senselessly. He remembered abandoning his duties, ignoring his siblings and his parents. He remembered trying to hurt Eliya, trying to use her for himself. He remembered his fight with March. Distraught, he sat up and crawled over to his sack. Reaching in, he felt around for the small sheath that surrounded the knife his father gave him. The knife that he had confidently taken the night he found the cave. The same knife he used to test the blue flames. He unsheathed it and looked at its polished blade as it mirrored the starry sky above.

It is only fitting that you should use that knife. You used it to bury the cup before.

"I want you gone."

Then dig. You know where the pain is...

The shaman's words were echoed by the actusfie, *... before the actusfie had reached your heart.*

"Get out of me!" Alechi shouted, he clawed at his chest. "Just leave me alone!"

Are you stupid? Did you forget? We are one. Your heart is bound, and there is only one way to sever your bound heart. You know that do you not?

"I don't want to."

But you know you have to. You want to be rid of me that badly, then you have only one option.

He tested the point of the knife with his pointer finger and blood started to flow slowly out of its tip. Though he had barely touched the knife, the puncture it made was remarkably deep.

"Dad must have just sharpened this," Alechi noted.

Then it will be quick, you can end it all here.

"He gave this to me so I'd come home."

But does he want you home? He let you go so easily.

"He at least wants this back."

If that was true, would he have sent you away so easily with only a meager knife.

"He trusts the axuli."

Do you?

"I-"

You do not know, do you? Then what is the point of it?

Alechi wiped the blood on his shirt and crawled to rest his back against the tree. He pointed the knife toward his chest. But then he felt frozen. He wanted so dearly to rid himself of the spirit latched onto his heart yet he feared the pain of death.

Plunge it in quickly and you will find yourself free of me.

"I don't know if I can."

You know the blade is sharp. If you thrust it into your heart, blood, pain, and grief will trickle out and you will not have to deal with them anymore. You will not have to deal with this world anymore. The death will be swift and painless, like sleep.

"I can't." Alechi's arms fell in front of him and with it, the knife. He could barely hold his grip and the knife rolled from his fingertips to the ground.

Oh, but you can, remember? If you do not believe you can, you never will. Is that not what the shaman said? What was the other thing? 'If you don't believe in yourself, believe those who believe in you'? Believe! You can dig it out, but even better is that unlike burying a chalice, it is one swift motion. You actually have the tool for the job this time.

Alechi struggled to fight off the actusfie's words. He simply was not willing to fight it at this point. If the spirit was right and he could rid himself of the spirit without having to go all the way to Som Catre, not only would it be easier, but he could leave the world behind and a better place.

He played with the hilt of the knife with his fingertips and grasped it firmly again. He brought the knife back to his chest and it stayed pointed there. He took a few deep breaths.

You are ready. Breathe in and let it all out at once as you pull the knife toward yourself.

Alechi breathed in. He heard birds chirping as they made their way over to him. The noise they made was rapid and getting progressively louder.

Breathe out and leave this world behind, better than it was when your wretched self was born into it.

The actusfie continued to urge him, preparing Alechi to breathe his last breath. He felt completely powerless to fight the spirit. The birds were chirping loudly above him as they had a few nights ago. He remembered that last time they had refused to let him sleep, he had been chased by wolves.

Useless birds really. You will be rid of their annoying presence too, all you have to do is let go. Let the dagger sink into your chest and it will all be over. No more hiking in these forsaken woods. No more cutting yourself on sharp rocks. No more, well... you.

Alechi held the knife in front of him. *Or you...*

Then Alechi heard a whistle in the air followed by a firm *thud*. Just above his right shoulder, embedded within the tree, was an arrow. He dropped the knife in shock and stood up to see if he could spot where the arrow had come from.

"Don' move another inch der, lad," a gruff, deep voice said from beyond the river bank. "I didn' come all dis way fer ya ta jus' off yerself."

"Who are you?" Alechi said, fearful of the voice he could not yet place a face to.

"I should be da one askin' ya," the voice said. "Dem birds kep' naggin' me fer som'in', so I followed dem an' find ya 'ere." The voice was exhausted and annoyed. A tall, bulky man appeared on the other side of the bank. His hair and beard were gray and unkempt. His serious eyes carried deep, dark bags. He was clearly well aged, yet his shape was one built to dominate the woods if he so chose. "So, le'me ask ya. Who *are* ya?"

9

Dawn

The old man stood expectantly, holding his bow with an arrow notched already. The arrow was pointed down. The man was ready to fire in an instant should he need to, but waited for Alechi's answer over the sound of the water.

"I am Alechi," he finally answered.

"Al-ay-kai, was it? I'll stick wit' 'lad,'" The old man said, stressing each syllable of his name as he struggled to comprehend what parent would name their child like that. "Now, yer gon' pick up dat knife dere an' put dat cover back onit." Alechi was hesitant to listen to the man, partially because he could barely understand him, partially because the actusfie was whispering thoughts that only made him even more suspicious of a strange man who found him in the middle of nowhere in the woods following birds.

He's unpredictable and incomprehensible, just walk away. You don't need the knife, you still have the...

"Ay now, you best quiet down dere," the old man said with authority that felt similar to the shaman's in some way, but Alechi did not believe this man to be anything close to a shaman.

Who does he think he is? He's a crazy, old...

"I ain' crazy," the man said. Alechi was shocked, but too bewildered to say anything, so the man continued, "Now do as yer told. We don' exactly have too much time ou' 'ere 'fore dat thin's frien's start showin' up."

What is he even saying? He's just a luna-

"I said quiet." There seemed to be a little bit of power in the simple, stern words the man spoke. Alechi finally believed him to be worthy of his respect based purely on the tone of his voice. It was assertive, yet caring all at the same time, not unlike the shaman's, but definitely not the same. The spirit was quieted.

Alechi picked up the knife at last. The knife now felt strange to him, and he was wondering why he ever thought to use it. He sheathed it and looked to the man for more instructions.

"Good lad," the man said. "Now stay put, ya'hear? I be 'ight back." The man disappeared into the trees on the other side of the river and in a few moments returned carrying all by himself one end of a large log on his shoulder. The log was thick and long and left a gash in the earth as it dragged behind him. The man set the log down and wiped his hands briefly before running off behind it. Alechi heard a loud groan as the log was pushed across the river and soon a makeshift bridge was now between them. "Git o'er 'ere!"

Alechi was scared. He had underestimated this man again, first his worth, then his strength. The log was definitely thick enough to walk on, but Alechi did not even want to risk falling into the river. The man beckoned him again with his hand.

"Could... could you hold it?" Alechi asked. The man, even as exhausted as he was, smiled and bent over. He placed his hands on the log and nodded to Alechi. Then, Alechi gathered all of his gear and put it on his back again. He took one careful step onto the log, testing it for movement, but there was none. Soon, his next foot followed and he stood completely on the log, taking care to keep his balance. He kept his eyes on his feet and though there was plenty of room on the log for him to lie down without any concerns of falling off, he stayed as close to the center of the log as he shuffled over. Around the midpoint of the log, he slipped, risking a fall into the river but soon regained his balance.

"Don' be 'fraid, lad," the man said. "Eyes on me, not yer feet."

"What if I slip again?"

"Yer only gon' slip if ya keep worr'in' 'bout where ya put yer feet! Ya jus' gotta walk forward! Breathe an' look 'ere!"

Alechi took a few deep breaths and tried his best to focus on the man at the end of the makeshift bridge. Suddenly, the man stood up, much to the dismay of Alechi who now feared for his very life. He felt betrayed but before he could get a word out to protest, the old man's bow was around him and he was pulled to safety as he fell hard on the ground next to the old man.

"Took ya lon' 'nuff!" the man grunted.

Alechi groaned in pain from the fall, "Why did you do that?" He said, getting up and gripping the man's hand as it was offered.

"Well, ya did yer bes' gettin' dis far, figur'd I'd pull ya de res' o' de wey," the man said. "Ain' 'boutta risk ya doin' som'in stupid."

"I could have made it!" Alechi protested. "It was no more than...

eight feet!"

The old man looked up and down at Alechi then nodded to himself, "Yer shorter. Eider way I'd hafta cover 'bout two 'r three feet if ya fell forward." He looked carefully at Alechi again, "Yer jus' shy of six feet o' stupid. Like I said, ain' riskin dat." Though the man's words themselves were unclear and harsh, Alechi appreciated the directness.

"Do you have to call me stupid?"

"Are ya?"

"No?"

"Den why were ya boutta kill yerself?"

"That's... a long story..." Alechi said, trailing off.

"Izit?" The man said, doubtful of its length. "Yer gon' hafta tell me when we git back."

"Back where?"

"Ta my 'ouse! Where else! Y'ain't helpin' me thinkin' y'ain't stupid, lad." Though there was not much light this night, the old man wove through the trees as if it was broad daylight and there was not even shade. He helped Alechi over some of the trickier obstacles, almost shaming him for his lack of agility despite his youth.

"How do you see out here?" Alechi asked as the man helped him over a thick, fallen tree.

"I don' see much righ' now, I jus' know it ou' 'ere." The man replied as he grunted to lift Alechi with all his gear. "I spen' lotta time ou' 'ere, lad, I know it like de back o' my han'." The birds chirped above him. "Oh yeh, got dem too, followin some of deir warnin's of changes. An' when ya fall behin'."

"They aren't just birds?"

The old man stopped. Looked at Alechi for a moment then shook his head, "Nope." The man was almost confused, dumbfounded even. Then he muttered to himself, "No way he's dat stupid." The birds chirped above him.

"They aren't?"

"'Course dey ain't! Dis pair say dey been follwin' ya since yer village. Said ya asked fer help! I knew ya were stupid, lad, but... don'cha ever think?" He tapped his forehead with a few thick fingers.

"But I-"

The man held up his hand to interrupt him and his voice was straining to be polite, "Best if ya shut it fer a bit."

"Why?"

"Maybe I'll think yer less stupid."

Alechi stood still even as the man resumed walking. He was shocked at the direct insult and wanted to complain but figured he shouldn't. The pair walked in silence until they came to a small clearing with a hut within its borders. The residual coals of a fire, surrounded by a ring of rocks with a pot suspended from a simple structure above it, smoked and smoldered outside the hut. The aroma from the area reminded him of his mother's venison stew and the flowers nearby reminded him of the village gardens. It seemed to Alechi that despite his distance from Lagdin, almost everything there reminded him of home.

"Com'on in," the man said. "Take a seat any place ya like."

The inside of the hut was dark, but the man soon lit a torch to illuminate the walls with a dim, orange light. On the farthest side from the door was a bed. A table, seemingly big enough to prepare food on, stood next to the bed and a pair of chairs sat on either side of it. Closer to the door, there was a stone stove with a thin chimney above it. A bed of coals and ash underneath the metal rack glowed with faint remnants of heat. There were no windows in the dark hut and Alechi stood in the doorway, hesitant to move away from the starlight. The man grunted behind him, urging him to move and the man lit three more torches around the hut, placing the first one he lit in a holster beside the door. The room was brighter, but what Alechi noticed, and what was there, did not change. He continued to stand near the doorway until the man sat himself down in the chair closest to the bed with a loud exhale, as if letting all the wind in him out at once. He stared at Alechi for a few moments. "Ya gonna sit?"

"Oh, right," he responded, breaking from his trance in the doorway. He walked over and sat across from the man. "I don't even know your name."

"Do it matter to ya?"

"I mean, it is hard to talk to someone without a name."

The man snorted, amused by his response. "Rorick."

"Rorick?"

"Don'cha wear it out now, lad."

"Well, my name is Alechi," he replied, disappointedly. "In case you already forgot."

"Didn' forget, jus' didn' care."

Alechi frowned, "You asked for my name."

"I ask'd who ya are," Rorick corrected, "Don' care 'bout yer name."

"What do you mean? Aren't they the same?"

Rorick frowned disappointedly and sighed. "No, lad, dey ain't."

"Well then who are you?"

"Fair nuff," Rorick said. "I'll give you an example.

"I am a man, son of Treyran and Agnes of Shre village. I live in deese woods 'cause I know an' understand de axuli well, de actusfie too. Some axuli call'd me ou' here long ago, but I jus' follow deir lead an' dey ain't led me astray yet. Some days I miss my village, but I know it's best ta listen ta de axuli. If I'm bein' honest, I lost track o' how old I am now, ain't really important."

"Seems simple enough," Alechi said, nodding his head lightly.

"Dat was jus' de surface, lad," Rorick said, "Dere's a lot more ta me dan dat, but ya go ahead."

"Well, I am Alechi..." he started.

"Don' madder," Rorick interrupted, "but continya."

"I'm the first child of Jerald and Ezri of Lagdin village. I am on my way to Som Catre because I listened to an actusfie and now it is a part of me as well..."

"No it ain't," Rorick said firmly. "Keep goin'."

"I got lost in these woods and I can't seem to find my way out. I am fourteen winters old, soon to be fifteen. I'm a terrible brother to my sisters, even worse to my brother, I don't even remember the last time I spoke to them." The pace of his words was quickening, but there were longer pauses between each sentence, he could not help but let loose the words he spoke.

"Don' make ya terrible."

"I'm alone."

"Y'ain't."

"At this point, I am no better than the actusfie, I've done horrible things to people."

"Hold on der, lad." The man stood up and walked over to the stove, set some small wood on it and started a fire, gradually adding more wood until he deemed it a suitable heat. He brought out a pot and waited for it to boil all while Alechi just watched.

"What are we waiting for?"

"Tea."

"Why?"

"Well wit' what ya jus' tol' me, I figure we gonna be here a while," Rorick answered. "May as well have som'in ta drink."

"If I'm being honest, I'd rather just sleep."

"Den use de bed if ya like, more tea for me den. We can talk in de mornin'," he shrugged. "But firs' I gotta ask ya, why did ya want my name if y'ain't gonna use it?"

Alechi looked at Rorick for a second, who was minding himself as he made the tea. "I'm not sure," he answered at length, "I think it is just nice knowing the name of the person who saved me."

Rorick scoffed in amusement again, "An' why's dat?"

"Just in case I ever need your help again," Alechi continued before rolling himself onto the hay mattress at the end of the hut and falling asleep in a near instant. Rorick stayed up for a little while longer, minding his own business as he sipped his tea and waited for the torches to burn out over the hour. Then he settled himself into a chair and slept until the morning.

Despite going to sleep last, Rorick woke up first and went outside to gather some wood so he could start a fire for a stew. He gathered some various leaves and nuts from nearby trees and bushes and some vegetables he had from storage. He went to a stream not too far off, an offshoot from the river Alechi had crossed the night before, and combined all the ingredients into a single, profoundly pleasant smelling stew. The scent of the stew stirred Alechi from his slumber. He was tired of the simpler foods he had been eating along the road.

Rorick saw him moving and said gruffly, "So yer fin'lly awake! Took ya long nuff."

Alechi groaned as he forced his eyes open, "Sorry. I haven't had many chances to sleep lately."

"Don' pologize, lad," Rorick said. "Restin' is key to gettin anywhere."

"Thank you," Alechi said as he graciously accepted the bowl of stew offered. Though the bowl was hot, it felt pleasant considering the morning cold.

Rorick sat down in one of the chairs and began to sip quietly from his own bowl of stew. "So, 'ow about we git started with you tellin' me 'ow you got 'ere."

"That's a long story." Within Alechi's voice was a hint of shame, defeat, and shyness. He did not want to relive any of what he had gone through and was still strangely unsure about Rorick.

"I got time," Rorick assured him.

Alechi told Rorick the whole story of how he had met the actusfie, treated his family and friends after, and how he got lost in the woods. "Then, while I was cornered, I... I don't know, I couldn't move, I had room to run, but I felt cornered as the wolves drew near. But then that rabbit jumped across and died, and I just watched. I couldn't move. Once I finally did start to move thanks to those axuli I realized just how worthless I am. I couldn't even stop one of those wolves if I tried, and well, as you know I did."

Rorick waited patiently for him to continue, sipping his stew to keep himself busy.

Alechi, feeling uncomfortable with the silence, sighed out, "Well that combined with how horrible I've been to others, my own worthlessness, and getting this damn thing out of me, is what led me to want to, you know."

"All right, lad," Rorick finally started, "I wanna run tru some of these events with you again, namely when dat 'rabbit,' also an axuli, in case you were dumb nuff to miss dat one too, jumped in front of de wolves."

"What about it?"

"Ya said dat made you feel worthless, but ya got it backward!"

Alechi's confusion spread across his whole face.

"Deh axuli sacrificed itself for ya, lad," Rorick announced excitedly. "Got any 'dea how lucky y'are?"

"I mean I am lucky to be aliv-"

"Mo'e dan dat! Look, axuli are more dan jist beenevolen' spirits, dey are *good* spirits, dey 'fend everythin' in creation dat is held dear, yes, but dey can do dat just by existing. Dat axuli sacrificed itself for ya because you are worth something. It coulda lived forev'r, it coulda run away, it coulda just sent dose actusfie away, but it laid itself down for ya so dat dey would stop huntin' you. Doze wolves'll likely never have nother meal like it."

"I don't know, it could have just been to protect the other ones that were with me, the birds."

"Did ya...? Did you even listen to a word I jist said?" Rorick pinched the bridge of his nose. "Dem birds weren't in danger, needer was de rabbit, dey did it for you. Dey believe dat you can, no... dey know you can, I would say ask dem yourself, but dat is a skill dat takes time and practice with axuli ev'ry day at all times of the day."

"But why would they? I am not a life worth-"

"Don't ya finish dat sentence," Rorick interrupted sternly. "Else I might start thinkin' yer deaf too. Who cares what ya did? Sure, ya can't always fix whatev'r ya did in de past, but yer life is still worth it, lad! Yer giv'n such a great gift to have un die for ya. Don't trivialize it to 'em dyin' for anyone else."

"I can't do anything right, though!" Alechi retorted, refusing, yet desiring, to believe Rorick's words. "How can they believe in me when I can never do anything right? Anytime I try I screw up? I've turned them away again and again and again, why do they keep coming back?" Alechi was on the verge of tears, so he hid his face in his arms.

"'Cause, Alechi, like yer parents, de axuli love ya, as dey do all thin's. Much like how yer parents likely can't decide 'tween you and yer siblings who deir favorite is, so it is wit' dem."

"That's stupid," he said bluntly. Rorick said nothing. So Alechi continued, "I can't do it, though, I can't get rid of this damn actusfie."

Rorick shook his head affectionately, "Why d'ya think yer on dis journey? Have confidence in de fact dat ya made it dis far, have confidence in dose supportin' ya, in de axuli. Dey've helped you dis far haven' dey? If ya have faith dat dose supporting ya, the axuli, dose dat b'lieve in ya, can keep pushin' ya forward no matter what, you'll be confident in yer ability to get it done. Dey won't leave ya alone. Trust me, dose birds wouldn't shut up 'bout ya."

"I don't know how to move forward."

"Let dem lead ya," Rorick said.

"I can't fight actusfie either, I was stupid to even try, I don't want to feel worthless."

"Well, yer right dat it was stupid for ya ta try on yer own, but now y'aren't. Long as ya cooperate with dem, I know de axuli'll keep ya safe. So safe dat you'll never have to draw dat sword and buckl'r 'til it's time for ya ta strike down de actusfie wit'in ya."

"Have you done it before?"

"Lad, anyone dat's lived has fought a' actusfie, some are jist a littl' tuffer dan others. Yers happens ta be a tuffer one."

"Oh..."

"Hey, lad, it's gon be 'ard, you'll be challenged, you'll be temp'ed to jis give up, but if ya trust de axuli at yer side, you'll win, dat I can promise ya."

Rorick continued to assure him for some time. Then, around mid-day, he said, "Come on, I want yer help with somethin'."

"What?"

"Come 'n see."

"I'm hung-"

"I know," Rorick said, mid-toss. "Eat dat."

"Thanks," Alechi said, catching a tough, well-seasoned, piece of jerky in his hands. Its taste was as familiar as it was gamey. It was stag meat. He followed Rorick in the broad daylight, finding the forest to be beautiful in the dazzling daylight, especially compared to the shrouded darkness of night. He recognized some of the area as the place they had passed through last night and the sound of rushing water was soon heard. They were back at the river and the log was still in place.

"Git my arrow back fer me."

It took Alechi a moment to process what was just requested before he protested with a simple, "What?"

"Git my-"

"I know what you said, but I almost died last time, I don't want to risk that again."

"Oh, but please," Rorick said mockingly, "I'm too old ta do it myself and arrows are a littl' difficul' ta make wit my old weak hands." Though Rorick was perfectly capable of retrieving the arrow, and his hands were strong and firm, the point he made was clear enough.

"Fine," Alechi said hesitantly. He placed a foot up onto the log. "Will you at least hold it again?"

"Do ya trust me?"

"Do you want an honest answer?"

He nodded.

"No."

"Well, trust me, you'll be fine, nothing'll happen t'ya. Jis keep yer eyes forward, focus on de oder end of de log an' you'll be fine. Have some faith in yerself." Rorick pounded his chest with a fist once and puffed out his chest, a childlike display of his own confidence.

Alechi took a deep breath and started walking, keeping his eyes focused on the far end of the log, and though he moved at a slow pace, it was steady and he made it to the other side in no time. He pulled the arrow from the tree where he nearly killed himself, finally allowing himself to look back at Rorick who was standing nowhere near the log. "I thought you said you would hold it!" He shouted fearfully.

"I didn' say dat!" Rorick shouted back. "Ya did dat all on yer own! Confidence is key to victory, lad, an' dat's de firs' time I've seen ya have confidence since we met."

Alechi considered it for a moment and was amazed at himself, he assured himself again that he could make it across the log, stepped up, focused on the other end and started moving, then he started moving faster across, confident he could make it even faster, he slipped near the end of the log and grabbed onto it as the water teased his feet. He could not pull himself up back onto the log, but Rorick stretched out his hand. Alechi grabbed Rorick's hand and was pulled to safety.

"Don' overdo it, lad. When confidence 'comes pride, it is yer enemy." He paused for a moment, allowing Alechi to reflect on the words. "Now, let's head back," he continued, "I got some mo'e work for ya 'fore I send ya on yer way."

10

Forward

Alechi was instructed to simply do as the old man did. He stayed with the man for about a week. On his last day with the man, he helped Rorick gather some extra supplies to restock the food he had consumed, helped carry large buckets of water to the hut, cut some wood and empty the traps. It was a mostly silent endeavor with the only exceptions being the axuli chirping above them and a few words of guidance and direction such as, "grab dose buckits," or "check o'er dere."

"All done," Alechi said after finishing what he was told would be his last chore.

"Good job, lad," Rorick replied. "Now I got nother question fer ya. Notice anythin'?"

Alechi started to look around, "Yeah, we got a lot of food, my hands are sweating despite the cold, and I'm tired."

"Dat all?"

He looked around even more intensely, trying to find some kind of hidden gift or at the very least something worth noting. "The birds?" he asked.

"You askin'?"

"The birds," he said, removing the question from his previous answer. "Or I guess I should call them axuli."

"Right. Nothin' else?"

Alechi was starting to get frustrated. What was it that he wasn't noticing? Or rather what was it that Rorick wanted him to notice? "You... trimmed your beard?" But the old man's beard was still as unkempt as ever.

"Oh, danks fer noticin'!" Rorick fake blushed, brushing it with his hand. Then he shouted, unsure how he could have encountered someone so dense, "No, I didn' trim my beard! Think 'bout yerself!"

"I mean that's the first time in a long time I've done so many things in a day..."

"And...?" Rorick attempted to lead.

"And I feel stronger."

"And...?" He tried again, desperately straining his voice.

"I... I don't know! Okay? What should I be noticing?"

"What's been missin'?"

Alechi groaned in frustration, as he often did whenever the actusfie would speak to his mind, but that's when it struck him. He hadn't heard from the actusfie in a while. Even when he was with the shaman, the actusfie liked to speak up whenever it felt like it even if it knew it could be silenced. "It's quiet." Alechi placed his hand over his heart, confused at the reason as to why. He wondered how Rorick had gotten it to be quiet for so long. He thought aloud to himself, "Is it gone?" Then aloud and more excitedly, "Does this mean I can go home?"

"'Fraid not, lad," Rorick answered for him.

"Then why is it so quiet?"

"Ya didn' give it any time or anythin' ta go off of," Rorick answered. "Actusfie thrive on de despair of oders an' dey love ta cause it, but because yer so occupied workin' dese chores, even dough some would and some have whined 'bout it, you were doin' somethin' you were capable of doin'."

"You didn't hush it?"

"I never did, lad," Rorick responded sincerely. "I'm sure someone's told ya dis before, but the only one who can control dat thing right now is you."

Alechi chuckled lightly to himself as he recalled the shaman's words, "Yeah, you're right."

"Ya still got a long way 'head of you, but now dat ya know you can shut dat thing up, de road should move fasta for ya."

"But how? How am I supposed to get rid of it?"

"Yer goal should be ta get rid of it, dat's good," Rorick affirmed, adding, "but ta keep it quiet, don' think of gettin' rid of it. If you think of dat, it'll become louder dan it was b'fore. Fer now, keepin' yerself busy is a good firs' step. Keep yerself busy with good honest work, not jist anythin'll keep it away. I can't get rid of it. I can't pull it outta ya, you gotta push it out. Dey'll teach ya dat up in Som Catre."

"Why can't you just teach me?"

"I know de 'what' and dey know de 'how', that's all it is. I can get ya started, make it shut up a little, but actually gettin' rid of it, I don' got a clue."

"Oh," Alechi said defeatedly. He started wondering how he would fare on the road alone without Rorick nearby to aid him, wonder turned to worry and doubt.

"Don't."

He's right, you should keep your head up, the actusfie taunted, after all you held me off for what? A mere day? Compare that to the entire year I-

"Shut it," Rorick said, "Do it yerself."

Alechi tried thinking of other things, shutting his eyes tightly as he tried to think, but the actusfie had pulled his entire attention. Though his eyes were shut, he thought he could see roaring flames of a village, one that looked much like Lagdin, burning it to the ground.

If you don't go back, that will be your end.

"Think of de axuli!" Rorick demanded. The old man's worry grew. He did not know what the actusfie had shown Alechi, but it was clear it was trying to turn him astray.

Think of your family, of March, then in a voice as sly and cunning as a snake it suggested, *of Eliya.*

"I- I have to go back!" Alechi stammered out. His eyes opened and he started to panic, frantically searching for a way past Rorick, but the old man, despite his age, stopped him no matter how fast Alechi considered himself to be. Rorick had the advantage of a calm mind after all. "Get out of my way!" Alechi demanded.

"Quiet!" Rorick commanded the spirit with a harsh voice. He held Alechi tightly within his strong grasp, restricting his movement, but Alechi kept kicking and screaming, trying to free himself. "Quiet." Rorick said again, softly. "'Member de warm 'arth."

The flames held within Alechi's eyelids dimmed.

"'Member de sacrifice."

Now before his eyes was a well-contained hearth, nothing but the hot coals coated in white ash warming his body during a cold winter night.

"Ain't enti'ly wrong to think of fam'ly, but if de choice is 'tween family and dis quest you're on, finish it first, den see your family. Dey can be yer motivation."

Alechi opened his eyes at last, and he saw the world as it was, no hearth, and no raging flames. His breathing slowed and he calmed down. "I miss them."

"Aye, as 'ould any'un. You'll see 'em ag'in," Rorick said, sympathetically. "Now, let's git ya movin'. We oughtta make it ta Shre 'fore sunset."

They began their walk, and as it was with most things they did together, it was silent between them. Alechi had less need for direction as he simply followed Rorick along the path he tread before him, so the axuli, the river and the wind were the only causes for noise. The trail Rorick led them through was far less linear than Alechi would have hoped, and he found himself looking through the trees to occasionally see a landmark he had passed earlier, wondering why they had to take such a roundabout way. The woods were far less frightening now that he was travelling with Rorick.

He saw now what he failed to see before: a piece of home. The trees, even the grasses, were all similar species to those around Lagdin, yet it also reminded him of how much farther he had to go. Som Catre was still hundreds of miles away, and it seemed to him that he would never reach those walls, especially if he went alone. He hoped Rorick would come with him, but the old man had made it clear it was only to the village, then they would part ways.

When they finally came to Shre from a hill above the town, Alechi recognized even more aspects that reminded him of home. They, like Lagdin, had a circular set up but on a much larger scale. Shre was a much busier town and there was an established ring of stalls for their much busier market. There were more than just high priced items there for suitors, everything from food to clothes to simple toys were covered by the traders in their common area. An irrigated stream fed into a small pond on the side of the city and another stream was used to drain excess water and fed it back to the river Alechi had followed earlier. The water in the pond was clear enough to see through to the bottom. In the daylight, the town glittered like a chest of gems in the sun.

Rorick led him to the center of the village and told him to stay put as he went to go talk with some of the merchants. Alechi stood in wonder at the sight of the bustling town center and though he recognized no one, nor others him, he was greeted with kindness by everyone who passed him by. He found the inclusion of cobblestone pathways in the town center remarkable. Horses and wagons bustled over the pavement. After some time and the brief exchange of formalities, Rorick returned with a merchant following him.

"Dis is 'im," he said, gesturing lightly toward Alechi.

"Evening, Alechi," the merchant said, his tone was polite. "I am Tesvi." He offered a handshake.

Alechi accepted it. "Nice to meet you."

"I hear you need a ride to Som Catre, and fortunately for you, I am making my way there."

Alechi nodded. "What do you need me to do?"

"I paid 'im and promist you'd 'elp defend 'is cargo," Rorick explained.

And with a genuinely soft smile on his face, Tesvi teased Alechi, "And I expect you to be a great defender." He held an invisible sword and made a few dramatic swings. Then he lifted his wide-brimmed cloth hat to fix his hair underneath before placing it back on his head. "Come Alechi, I'll show you to the wagon and show you where you will be during the ride." He seemed to be a joyful, professional man.

"I'll see ya 'round, lad," Rorick said, "I'll tell 'em to watch o'er ya, an' dey will be, I know it." Then Rorick began walking back to his home deep in the woods.

Alechi followed Tesvi for a few steps before asking for a moment, he ran to Rorick and tapped the stout man on his shoulder and initially offered a hug before the two of them awkwardly shifted to a handshake. "Thank you," Alechi said. While he did not yet cry, tears lingered in his eyelids and his voice was strained.

"Only doin' my job... Alechi," he responded, carefully pronouncing the name. "Now git goin', dwellin' ere won't do ya any good." Rorick patted Alechi's shoulder and pushed him back toward the town. Alechi nodded and started walking back while Rorick watched with a smile.

Alechi returned to Tesvi and was led to the back of a wagon. Painted on the fabric cover of the wagon on either side was an emblem with a prominent "T" and a treasure chest behind it enclosed within a circle. He took off his sword and buckler and set them inside the wagon before climbing inside himself. The inside of the wagon was filled with all sorts of goods, some foods, many like the ones he had seen at home: potatoes, carrots, among other root vegetables. Near the front of the wagon was an assortment of jerky, salted pork, some wheels of cheese sealed in wax and wrapped in burlap, and a small wooden chest that Alechi could only imagine was filled with coins.

"I am not sure if you know this, Alechi," Tesvi said, "but Shre is actually very famous for its cheese, it is very popular in Som Catre."

Alechi's stomach grumbled, even though he had a hearty meal earlier that day with Rorick, "It certainly looks good."

"I always buy some for myself and a lot more to sell, would you like some?" Tesvi offered. He opened one of the burlap sacks that had cheese, revealing that it had already been cut into, and cut a piece off for himself and put it in his mouth. Savoring the taste with bliss, he looked to Alechi who nodded. Alechi accepted another piece as Tesvi cut one off and took a small bite of the slice, the cheese was crumbly and dry but very soft. The deliciousness of the cheese bled through Alechi's expression.

"Addicting, isn't it?"

"Yes," Alechi said, stuffing the rest of his slice into his mouth. "Can I have another?"

"You are welcome to help yourself, just don't eat all of it," Tesvi said, "Too much of this cheese and you won't be able to move to defend the wagon."

"Then I think I will hold off."

"That seems wise," Tesvi agreed, lightly chuckling. He walked around to the front of the wagon and reined the horses to the wagon, harnessing them before climbing up to the seat at the front. "We have only a few hours of daylight left, but we should be able to easily make it to the next village before nightfall. Are you ready to go?"

Alechi hesitated for a moment, looking out the back and thought of home, and March.

Well? Are you?

"Shut up," he whispered to the actusfie. Then he thought to himself whether he could do it, whether he really could leave it all behind. It would be harder to turn back while he rode in a wagon, he wondered whether he was willing to give that opportunity up. He shook the doubt away and responded, "Ready."

With a sudden jerk, the wagon started moving and rattling with every bump in the road. The wooden wheels squeaked as they turned and the horses' hooves hit hard against the cobbled ground with every step, softening only once they reached the dirt road outside Shre.

The journey was slow and the road was wide. Alechi spent most of his time looking out the back of the wagon as the sun fell past the tree line. Nothing even seemed to dare approach the road.

"How often do they show up?" Alechi called back. When he didn't get an answer he moved through the back of the wagon to where Tesvi was seated to repeat his question.

"Truth be told, the closer you get to Som Catre, the safer it is," he answered. "Dangers in this area are pretty rare. It is good of you to be vigilant, but your protection will hardly be necessary."

Alechi furrowed his brow and then asked what seemed to be the obvious question, "Well then why are you taking me?"

"You need to get to Som Catre don't you? I am headed there anyway," then he smiled. "And it never hurts to have someone else to talk to."

"How much did Ror-"

"A single copper piece. Don't worry, I have no intention of robbing a man like him."

"Because he's poor?"

"Because he helps people," Tesvi said. "That's enough for me. But he insisted on payment, so I took the copper and that was it."

With that, Alechi relayed to him stories from back in Lagdin about his friends and his many adventures and dramatic duels with March. It was a welcome interaction considering how much Rorick preferred silence. Tesvi was a good listener, and though their conversations were shallow, it comforted both of them. Tesvi shared some of his own stories of his trades.

"Once, while I was trading in a village near Som Catre, I was approached by a pair of children. They asked if I had anything they could buy and I showed them all of my wares. I showed them some toys I had brought from Som Catre, some food, plenty of sweets, you know? I showed them anything and everything a kid could want, even some toy swords..."

"My friends and I were stuck with sticks and pot lids! I would have liked one of those."

"I know right? But do you know what they picked instead?"

"What?"

"They asked to buy a leaf that had fallen onto one of my products," Tesvi said, failing to hold a straight face as a smirk escaped his will.

"Why?" Alechi asked, his face scrunching in an attempt to

rationalize the children's thought process.

"I don't know, I just gave it to them for free. I was baffled myself, I thought maybe they were pointing at the thing underneath the leaf, but when I double checked, it was the leaf they wanted. I watched them run away as if it was the rarest leaf in the world. Anyway, I thought that was an adorable moment." He looked ahead, "Oh, we're almost to our first stop, Ingled."

The sun had just barely sunk below the horizon on their left, leaving only a haze of gray light, the brightest of stars, and the dim fires of lamps from the village ahead. They were stopped at the gates briefly for the guards to check the wagon, cross-checking it with an inventory list Tesvi supplied. The book he supplied was ragged, the edges of the paper inside were torn and wrinkled from use.

Once they were cleared, they were welcomed into the village and its local shaman led them to an inn before retreating to his own home somewhere in the village. As they passed through Alechi noticed that the center of the village was similar to his own in that the markets were there, but the shaman's home seemed to be elsewhere. Alechi thought it strange that visitors did not stay with the shaman or with families, but he supposed with enough business coming through the town, it might be too difficult.

Tesvi and Alechi brought the wagon to the innkeeper's care where he assured them everything would be safe with him. Another man took the horses to the inn's stables.

"Are you hungry?" Tesvi asked. "Ingled is known for its spiced venison."

Alechi hadn't even considered food ever since he had that cheese, but a weak grumble from his stomach assured the pair everything they needed to know. Tesvi paid the innkeeper for some freshly cooked venison, and the two of them ate together. Alechi felt at ease.

As it was still early into the night, they sat around the inn's roaring hearth and started swapping stories with the other merchants and travelers that had stopped in. "I killed a dragon once!" One of the mercenaries boasted with a hiccup. "It was a great green dragon," his arms flailing about to make broad gestures of size, "and it was attacking a village down south, you know how they like the colder weather, and I took a huge iron spear and frew it hard, it went *woosh* through the air an then *thud* righ through the dragon's neck."

"I'm from a village in the south, and I've never seen a dragon," Alechi said.

The man stood up, and stared at Alechi for a moment before stretching out his arms, "'Course you haven'! I killeded the dragon." He took a long drink from his tankard even as his words became progressively slurred, "You're welcome fer that by the way. Good old, Algoro ta thank fer that." He patted his chest. "Heero of Retarrrrannn!"

Alechi chucked, "Thanks, I guess."

"And for that story," Tesvi said, then aside to Alechi, "though its truth is questionable," and then back to the mercenary, "I will get you another beer." Tesvi's generosity continued to warm Alechi's heart more than the fiery hearth ever could.

Another person chimed in, who Alechi judged to be a wealthy merchant based on the clothing he wore, "Where are you from in the south?"

"Lagdin."

"Lagdin, wow," the merchant's eyes widened and he nodded his head for a little bit. "What are you doing all the way up here?"

Alechi started to get nervous. If he told them he was on his way to get rid of an actusfie, they might kick him out of the inn, and Tesvi, who was still at the bar just in earshot, might not let him ride in the wagon with him anymore.

Well... what are you doing here?

"I don't know," Alechi said aloud in response to both questions he had been asked.

"Well if you want, I am headed down to Lagdin, I will bring you along if you would like. Are you any good with that sword of yours?"

"Hey! Thas what you hired me for!" Algoro cried out, followed by a belch filled with the stench of cheap alcohol.

"I would say you could learn from him, but I would also advise against it," the merchant said to Alechi. "And you," the merchant turned frustratedly toward the mercenary, "you will still have your job, I am just offering this kid a way home."

"Good," the mercenary said, "I ain' gonna be shown up by some kid." Then he fell backward onto the floor. Some of the other mercenaries carried him back to his room as Tesvi returned from the bar.

"What happened to him?" Tesvi asked, carrying another tankard full of beer.

The wealthy merchant replied, "Too many people buying him drinks," but he and Tesvi smiled at each other before the merchant brought the conversation back to Alechi. "So, what do you say? You want a ride back to Lagdin? Free of charge."

Alechi looked to Tesvi for an excuse, but his current companion shrugged, "Up to you, I'm not going to stop you."

Come on, you've been gone long enough. You wasted enough time with that haggard in the woods, people will probably think you're already finished anyway! You could just go home and be welcomed as a hero! Think about it, don't you want to see your family? Your friends? Or are they just worthless to you? Don't you want to go back? Wouldn't it be so much easier, too? No one would even notice I'm still here, you could blend right back in.

The actusfie's words seemed to be coming at him faster than he could even think of the word "quiet." He thought of his family and his friends and how he could hurt them if he returned before he had finished what he had set out to do.

I promise you wi-

"I am sorry, sir, I have something I need to take care of in Som Catre," Alechi said firmly, "So I'll stick with Mister Tesvi here."

11

Determination

"*Som Catre?*" The wealthy merchant said, leaning back, eyes widening while an impressed frown spread its way across his face, "That'll be a long road home! Well, I hope you are able to get back safely."

"I almost can't wait."

"I'd imagine... Hey, I never asked, what was your name?" The merchant asked, pulling out a small notebook and charcoal pencil.

"Alechi. Yours?"

"Draydric," the merchant offered, noting the boy's name in one of the pages. "Alechi, eh? I'll let your shaman know you're safe when I get there. I assume he *knows* you are not in the village?"

"Yes, he saw me off."

"Good, good," the merchant said, nodding. "I am going to get some rest. I will need extra sleep if I am to deal with that drunkard all day tomorrow. Good night." He turned to Tesvi, "Thank you for the drinks, friend."

Tesvi and Alechi bid the wealthy merchant a good night as well and, after exchanging a few more stories with some of those still near the warm hearth, they too retired for the night.

The next morning, and until about midday, Tesvi sold some of his various goods in the merchant's circle, then the pair set off on the road again. The back of the wagon was certainly emptier. With fewer stories the two were willing to share with one another, the pair would take turns spotting creatures between the trees and pointing them out to each other. Unfortunately for them, that game soon also brought upon boredom and they were left to each other's silence. Occasionally, they would cross paths with another merchant and exchange greetings as the carts passed by. The trees on the side of the road gradually grew more sparse and the terrain between the towns rockier. The mountains of the capital were now in sight. The cart traveled on wider and wider roads as roads to and from various villages and towns converged. As night approached, they once more came upon a village.

"Ah, the last village before we reach Som Catre, at least on our route, Nauga," Tesvi said as he seemed to reminisce. In the glow of the sunset, the river of Aiman shone brilliantly as a beacon for them to follow. The village was just on the other side of a wide and long stone bridge that was rather empty at the present. Tesvi assured Alechi the bridge was normally busier with the comings and goings of traders. "We are getting in a little later than I hoped, but I suppose I am to blame for that. I took too long this morning," he said, then he looked at Alechi. "And maybe I should have had a little less food during our lunch." Tesvi patted his belly with content and smiled.

"Maybe," Alechi said, chuckling.

The paved bridge was incredibly smooth and the masonry and ornate carvings on its ramparts were beautiful beyond any initial impression. Carved into the stones were flowers, faces of old kings, vines, rivers, familiar creatures—stags, rabbits, and birds big and small—and just about anything Alechi could have imagined. Far below them, in the waters of Aiman, the river crashed against the base as it flowed rapidly underneath, drowning out the sounds of almost everything else.

Once again they checked with the guards at the gate and were welcomed in and Tesvi led the wagon straight to a particular inn in the town. Within Nauga, there were a few, but the one Tesvi chose for them was on the southern side, closest to the gate where they had just come in, and was called "The Riverside Recovery." The moment he walked in, the owner recognized him and it seemed he had a room set aside for the two of them already.

"The trick is..." Tesvi said, leaning over to Alechi and looking over his shoulder, "loyalty. I sell this man lots of food and in turn, he keeps a room ready for me whenever I need it."

The pair followed the owner to their room for the night. As both were exhausted from the long ride and bellies still full from their earlier meal, they elected to simply sleep the night away without worrying about anything going on in the nearby taverns.

At least, that was their intention. Tesvi went straight to sleep without a problem, but Alechi lay awake. He was thinking about how close he was to reaching Som Catre. He couldn't tell if he was more excited than he was scared. Though nothing on his face would show it, the reality was that he was more frightened than eager.

Have you ever considered that they wouldn't let you in?

"No," Alechi responded. "Now shut up." He shook his head as he had before to dispel the doubt.

It worked, the actusfie did not say anything else. That was until Alechi's mind wrapped back around to its question.

Isn't it obvious? It is a sacred city, do you really think they would let in someone with an actusfie?

"It's what I was sent for, of course they would."

Maybe. Maybe they only let people in with weaker ones. Their city is pure, is it not? Why would they taint it with you and me?

"No one has to know."

But what if they can tell? Even that haggardly old man could tell, so surely they can, too.

"I trust those that told me I should go."

But none of them have ever dealt with something like me, have they?

Alechi thought back to the shaman, to his mother, to Rorick and lastly looked over to Tesvi, and realized he never knew of them to struggle as hard as he had been struggling.

See? Maybe they can't let you in.

The thought festered in Alechi's mind for much longer than he liked. Much longer than anyone who loved him would have liked, though he did not perceive it. Then compelled by something flashing briefly in his memory of Rorick, he took a deep breath and let out slowly. "The axuli are on my side." He took another deep breath and said, "Now leave me be." After a few more breaths, he was fast asleep.

Waking up the next morning felt difficult for Alechi. Though in his mind, he was only kept awake for a few minutes by the actusfie, he felt like he needed another full night's rest.

Tesvi urged him out of bed. "Come on," he said, "we are headed straight for Som Catre after breakfast. The sooner we get moving the better."

Alechi rubbed his eyes and looked out their window, the daylight was already blinding even through the thin layer of curtains. "What time is it?"

"Still morning, but it'll be noon before we know it. Som Catre will be busy all day and I would prefer to beat the end of day rush."

Alechi got out of bed and put on the cloak and coat from home and wrapped his sword belt around his waist. Tesvi went to the innkeeper, handed him a couple of coins, and a hot breakfast of tea, biscuits, and sausage was soon before the merchant and the boy. The pair wolfed down their food and loaded the wagon back up with the more precious cargo they had removed the night before.

"All set?" Tesvi asked.

Alechi patted all his articles: cloak, coat, sword, shield and, after a few distressing pats, his father's dagger. He nodded.

"Okay, let's go," Tesvi said as he climbed up into the wagon and motioned for Alechi to do the same.

The morning had felt rushed and Alechi still desperately wanted to sleep, but, as the wagon was shaking violently with the speed Tesvi urged the horses, the best he could do was close his eyes and sit in the back, hiding from the sunlight.

Time passed quicker than he expected, and soon it was early afternoon. Tesvi called Alechi to the front. "This is your first time seeing Som Catre right?"

"Yeah," he replied, pushing aside the curtain to join the merchant on the wagon's seat.

He was struck by the city's beauty as they approached from the south. It sat between three mountain peaks and the sun shone clearly on the city's white stone and colorful banners. A tall keep nestled itself in the far back of the city closest to the meeting point of the three mountains. A bridge much like the one near Nauga decorated the pathway to the city. It crossed a man-made water channel diverged from the river to bring the fresh water closer and supply defense for the already seemingly impenetrable city. A pair of high watchtowers overlooked the entrance in the middle of the city's one wall, uniting the mountains. Beside the western border of the city, a dense forest of shimmering trees of all kinds stood proudly as it spanned for miles beyond the horizon. Farm land with a sea of wheat swaying in the wind covered the open flat plains to the east. As they approached, Alechi could clearly see now flags of green, blue, yellow and red displaying the same image of the head of a white stag with many antlers.

"Legend says that the city was founded by those that followed an axuli in the form of a white stag. It had gone to everyone who was scattered throughout Retaran and led them here."

"I've never seen a white stag before."

"No one's seen one since apparently. It left after the walls were built, but we are sure it is still watching over us, if not in the form of the stag then through all the other axuli."

They approached the gates and joined in a lengthy queue as guards checked the inventory of all those with wagons. Travelers with small packs or in some cases just their clothes and a walking stick walked by the line and right into the city without a second thought. The guards had swords and bucklers at their belts and studded helmets and armor. Each chest plate had the same stag. They held themselves high as they worked and the guards patrolling on the ramparts above the gates were armed with bows, keeping a watchful eye for anything amiss.

Inside, crowds of lowly travelers walked around and though the city had little room to breathe, not even a breath was heard.

When they finally arrived at the front, the guards asked for the cargo's inventory and Tesvi handed them a small leatherbound book open to a set page. Alechi now saw a third person approaching, an elderly man with a hand behind his bent back, a staff in his other hand, and eyes narrowed, staring at him. The man whispered something into the ear of one of the guards as they neared the end of the inventory list. The guard simply nodded and turned to Alechi.

"Son, would you mind stepping down for a moment?"

It's happening.

Alechi took the short leap down off the wagon and asked simply, "What's happening?"

The old man replied, his voice was firm, and though his eyes implied suspicion his words sounded genuine, "I just want to speak to you..." He held up his index and middle fingers just below his waist and mouthed, "two." Tesvi didn't notice.

He knows.

Alechi walked, looking down as he did, to the old man.

"You're free to go, sir," a guard said to Tesvi.

"Is everything okay with him? I have been tasked with getting him here so I would like to know if there is a problem."

"That will be for him to decide," the old man answered. He pulled Alechi further aside and into the walls of the city.

"Please move along, sir."

"I'll be at my shop, Alechi, it is in the third ring. You'll know it when you see it," Tesvi said. He turned to the guards now, "I expect to see someone there in the next hour, either him or one of you explaining to me why it isn't him." It was the first time Alechi heard Tesvi talk that aggressively, and to guards no less. Then the merchant whipped the reins and guided the horses into the busy streets.

"Come on... Alechi, was it?" The old man said, leading him into a watchtower.

The pair climbed a set of stairs that protruded from the wall and went up in a spiral. The man was careful to lean on the wall as he took each step one at a time. They stopped on a floor that just had a large, ornate wooden desk in the middle of the room and a couple of chairs to match. The old man motioned for Alechi to sit then sat himself down behind the desk.

"I suppose I should introduce myself. I am one of the shamans here. I am Shaman Exsanai," he said. "And I suppose you know why you were stopped?"

"Yes, I do," Alechi responded, feigning interest in the rather empty room to avoid eye contact. He did not want to see what he feared he would hear come from this shaman's lips.

"And why is that?"

"Because of *it*."

"What is it?"

If you are honest, they won't let you-

Alechi silenced the actusfie but his heart weighed his chest down, "An actusfie."

"Why have you brought it here? To the sacred city?"

"Because my shaman told me to come here."

"Is that all?"

There was silence. The rattling of wagons and the regular questions of the guards could be heard dimly below.

Exsanai waited patiently for a few minutes, never looking away from Alechi. Then he placed his hands on his arm rests and pushed himself up.

"If that's all, I'm going to have to ask you to leave."

Despite the absence of his friend, regularity had nearly completely resumed in Lagdin for March. In the midst of winter, there had been little time to play, not in the last few years at least. He and everyone else had duties to attend to, so he hardly thought anything of it. No amount of busyness could distract him from the thoughts of his missing friend. The adults never gave him a direct answer about what happened to him and the shaman, who normally was open about many things, kept discussion about Alechi very limited.

He remained hopeful that Alechi would soon return home. Every day, he passed the northern gate of Lagdin and climbed as high as he could to look for any sign of him.

Eliya remained mostly close to home, caring for her siblings from a place of safety and warmth. She had heard Alechi's apology and March often came to invite her out to play with the others, but she always refused. She had once thought Alechi wonderful, and if he could turn so rotten, she had no desire to surround herself with others like him. In the back of her mind, she knew she couldn't stay like this forever, but Alechi's form continued to loom over her in her nightmares.

Though she did not hate Alechi, she did not want him to come home. Not yet anyway. His apology had seemed genuine, but she needed more time. Eliya too checked the gate at least once a day to be sure she still had all the time she needed.

One particular day, about a week and a half after Alechi had left, a wagon accompanied by a pair of mercenaries approached the village. The children got excited, merchants were a rare sight at this time of year and they almost always had the finest of silver and gold jewelry, glass, and a limited supply of assorted weaponry. Whoever this merchant was, he would be the only one in the town at the time.

The shaman, upon hearing the children's sudden excitement, made his way to the north side of the village to welcome him. The children made a path for the shaman and most went back to their playing. March, however, was curious, so he stayed nearby.

"Ah, Draydric, I see you have come back!"

"Seeing as I seem to have a monopoly here every time I come, I don't see why I wouldn't!"

The mercenaries accompanying the cart walked past the pair of men as they laughed and made their way toward the center of the village. Lagdin was too small to have an inn or a tavern, but the village's families supplied all the necessary hospitality they could. Alechi's family was one of the first to step up.

Jerald approached one of the mercenaries, "We don't have much room, but one of mine is on an errand of sorts up north," the mercenaries' ears perked up, "so we have had a little extra food on our end if you would like any."

The mercenary took a close look at Jerald and asked while he continued to stare, feeling as though he recognized him, "How much would I owe ya?"

"Oh, nothing," Jerald replied kindly, "I'll take a little help in the morning chopping some wood if you'd like to pay me back, but it is not really necessary."

"Oh I'll help ya then, doesn't feel right not doin something," he said. Then he turned and shouted, "Hey Draydric!"

"Well I don't have enough room for all of—"

"This ain't about that," he interrupted, as he started walking back toward the merchant. "Draydric!"

After some explaining between the merchant, the shaman, and Jerald. Jerald said, "I have to go! I have to go tell Ezri and the others." Nothing could stop him. Nothing can stop a father like Jerald when he hears good news of his son.

The shaman smiled as he watched Jerald sprint to his humble home. Then he turned to Draydric and Algoro, "Thank you for letting me know. He left here about a week and a half ago. It is good to know he made it safely to some other villages and hopefully Som Catre."

"From what I have heard, and what I saw of the man myself, Tesvi seems to be a reliable fellow, especially among merchants," Draydric said. "I am sure he made it to Som Catre."

March was too excited by the news that his friend was okay to remember he was eavesdropping and came closer. His seemingly sudden presence gave a start to the visitors.

"Alechi is in Som Catre?" He asked the shaman just to be sure.

Unalarmed, the shaman answered, "Yes."

March was relieved for a moment, then something else dawned on him, "And you sent him out there, that far, alone?"

"In a way, yes."

"Why?"

"It is his journey to make."

"What do you mean?"

The visitors backed away from the conversation, leaving the shaman to deal with March alone as they followed Jerald and the other families.

"Alechi had a decision to make. Thus far he has been making the right choices, for the most part, to have made it as far as he did. He could have returned the day he left if he wanted to."

"Then why hasn't he?"

"Because, I hope, that he knows the importance of what he must do."

"Why couldn't you go with him?"

"I sent him armed and with some guardians, he does not need my physical presence. He has the lessons he was taught. If I was with him in the flesh, he may not feel he has a choice and then the entire journey would have been for naught. It is better this way. I have not abandoned him and I, too, eagerly await him; however, if he does not fulfill this journey for the sake of himself, the Alechi we once knew would be dead forever."

March understood little of this, but resigned himself to the idea that the shaman was being cryptic for a reason.

He wandered back to the north gate and spoke softly to the wild trees so they may bear his message to Alechi, "Make sure you tell me all about it when you get back."

12

Reflection

"What?" Alechi said, stunned. "No, I can't go back."

Exsanai walked to the door and was ready to descend the staircase. "Well why not? All your shaman told you to do was to come here and you don't seem to have any other reason. You're here aren't you? So you can go. I can't let an actusfie roam free in the city. That is my duty."

"I can't. I can't go back, not yet, I need to get rid of it."

Exsanai's ears perked up subtly, stopped his descent down the staircase and asked, "And why do *you* need to get rid of it?"

"I..."

"Well if you don't have an answer, then you don't need to. I'll have the guards escort you out and another guard will go tell your friend Tesvi that your business is resolved."

"Please, don't."

"Then give me a reason why *you* are here."

He won't take any answer you give him. You'll never get rid of me.

"SHUT UP!"

His shout brought a sudden silence. There were a few moments where it seemed there would and could be no other noise for the rest of eternity.

Ha. Look at what you've done. You'll never be let in now.

Then Exsanai broke through with a quiet, simple, and contemplative, "Why?" The noise outside resumed. Alechi did not respond. Exsanai sighed and resumed his descent down the tower taking the steps one at a time. Just out of Alechi's sight he stopped and waited.

Alechi felt his heart sink low and a lump formed in his throat. He opened his mouth to speak but no words came out, just lurches full of strained tears. The boy far from home fell to his knees and thinking he was alone let himself cry.

You're pitiful.

"Why won't you just leave? Why can't I get rid of you? Why

won't they help me? You're killing me from the inside out. Get out of me already!"

Doomed the moment you had that first taste.

"And therein lies our answer," Exsanai said, rising up a few steps. "*You* want it out. It is *killing* you."

"Wasn't that obvious?" Alechi choked out.

"Not to you it would seem. Not to you indeed."

"Of course I knew it," Alechi said, straining himself with every word to resist the urge to stand up and punch the shaman who was drawing ever nearer.

"Then why couldn't you answer me?"

"I... don't know."

"I think you do, but if you would allow me, or prefer me, to answer it for you, I can."

"Please do." Alechi's voice was beginning to restore itself back to normal as he regained his breath and temperance.

"What it is that I think you already know is this: that actusfie clouds your mind. All it ever does is lie. And it is quite successful in doing so because the way in which it lies is by telling you lies that seem to be true.

"The fact is that it cannot control you, only you can control you. No, don't blame yourself for what you have done. Do not blame yourself for not understanding the answer before. While that thing still dwells within you, it will always seem to have a certain sense of control over you by taking over in the areas where you lack. It targets your highest strengths and your lowest weaknesses leaving the best parts of you feeling like mediocrity and the worst feeling like atrocities. But do not believe these lies that it tells you. As you learn to identify your strengths and your weaknesses you will be better prepared to face it; however, if you wish to master anything beyond yourself, you must master yourself first.

"What I was asking of you, in identifying your own reason for being here, is a start toward self-mastery. Acknowledgement of your reality and a recognition of what is at stake. Before beginning any task, you must first know why you want to do it. Otherwise, in doing something for a reason which you do not know, you will find yourself failing to meet its end."

"But what if when my parents tell me to do something, and I don't know why? Should I just disobey them if I can't find the reason?"

"And from there we have another important lesson, because it is, as you say, that we must sometimes do things which we do not understand the reason for, but I will ask you a question first. Why did you ever listen to your parents? To your shaman back home?"

"Well when I was a kid, it was clear they loved me."

"Do you think they knew what they told you was better for you?"

"Maybe?"

"My guess would be so. Some experiences are harshly learned and can be taught by those who came before us so that following generations need not learn in the same harsh way. Though it should not be a source of despair if you must be the one to learn the lesson on your own. Sometimes, the best way for us to learn is to suffer through it ourselves. Trials and sufferings teach the teacher, after all, but the teacher must also be able to practice what he has learned. Your parents and their experience taught you of the actusfie for this reason, in hopes to keep you from their grasp."

"My parents have dealt with actusfie before?"

"Maybe. Maybe it was them, maybe it was taught to them by the shaman. Maybe it was an ancestor or even a friend of an ancestor. We are not meant to live in this world alone, nor experience it alone. For if each of us were alone, none of us would survive. We learn for ourselves and for the sake of others. You were sent here by your shaman because he knew it was best for you."

"Well, why couldn't he help me back there? Why did I have to come here?"

"Whether you know it or not, you have changed on your journey here. It may not have been much, but likely just enough, based on what little I have heard, that you now know a little more of who you are and why this is your task."

"I am not sure I have changed."

"When you left the village, could you silence the actusfie on your own?"

"No."

"And now?"

"I suppose. Sometimes. But that doesn't feel like change. I mean it doesn't change the actusfie."

"All growth is change. All growth is a blessing. For now, just know that you have indeed changed. We will attend to all your questions sooner or later, though some may not need answers. I'll be sending a guard to Tesvi's shop to let him know you will not be joining him there but coming with me."

"You're going to help me then?"

"Of course. You need my help, and now that I have seen that you want help, I know that you can begin to accept mine."

"Thank you."

"You're welcome," he said with a nod. He motioned for him to follow down the steps. When they stood behind the gate again Exsanai wandered over to the base of the other watchtower and, through the open door, Alechi saw him talk to a guard and what appeared to be a slightly younger shaman wearing similar robes. The guard stood up and with all haste took one of the horses to deliver the message, as the other shaman took Exsanai's place at the gate. Exsanai then walked back to Alechi and led him through the city.

While they passed through the city center, a group of children were playing a game he did not recognize near the fountain that displayed a gorgeous marble stag with its headed pointed to some place in the distant sky.

The children seemed to gather into small groups based on whatever one of the other kids was calling out, seemingly mimicking animals.

"What are they doing?"

"They are playing a game—I would have thought that would be apparent," Shaman Exsanai answered. Alechi had stopped walking as he stared at the children of seemingly all ages playing together. He was wholly mesmerized. "You can play it with them another day, perhaps even later today. But let's keep moving for now."

"Right," Alechi said. Though he still felt drawn to the game, he followed the shaman deeper into the city. Alechi's mind began to flood with questions. None of the people he passed seemed to notice he was a stranger, though he could tell it was not out of resentment but because all were occupied in conversations of laughter with one another. Many of the people seemed like they had never worked or never needed to.

Then, as they climbed a hill to a keep between the three peaks, he wondered why they hadn't taken horses and how far he was from Tesvi's shop.

Lastly, as his focus returned to his own situation, he thought of a question to ask. If Rorick and his own shaman in Lagdin had understood to a degree what his actusfie had spoken, he did not understand why Exsanai had kept quiet when it spoke to him. "Why didn't you-"

"I needed to measure how much control you had of it already and how much it knew about you," Exsanai answered. "Though neither bit of information would have changed my mind to help you, it does change my approach. Luckily, you seem to have had a good mentor. Most who come here are not yet at the point of silencing it themselves. You have a good knowledge of the actusfie, it seems, but still little knowledge and control of yourself. That is where the actusfie try to take hold. In that weakness."

"Rorick was my mentor, do you know him?"

The shaman thought for a moment, "I do not recall a man named Rorick. Was he a shaman?"

"No, at least, I don't think so."

"Then I don't believe I have. But he must know a lot to be able to teach that to someone in your condition. I can see the shadow within you. It is that dense. But do not be discouraged, I've dealt with much worse."

The rest of the journey was completed in silence as they reached the keep. Many shamans were navigating the area, moving through the giant, wide-open entrance doors constantly, in and out as some were returning from ministering to the city and others just leaving for it. Alechi had never seen so many shamans in one place. Exsanai led him to a room that only had two chairs facing each other with an hourglass on a small table between them. A stained-glass window shed a myriad of colors onto the floor.

"Now," Exsanai said, offering Alechi a seat, "tell me how you got here. Do not hold a single detail back. Even the smallest thing may make the biggest difference in how I address this actusfie."

And so Alechi relayed his story once more while Exsanai listened patiently to each word, intentionally hiding any reaction so Alechi would not be deterred. Alechi recounted that he and March had the discussion that day about his ability to defeat an actusfie, and he laughed a little at himself knowing his present situation now and the seeming impossibility of it all. He told of how he encountered the actusfie in the water, the bunny, which he now understood was an axuli, that saved him. Then he explained how he hurt his friends and disregarded his duties as a brother and a son. He looked up after explaining this, expecting some form of disgust, but Exsanai's face remained neutral as he waited for Alechi to continue. Alechi explained his journey across Retaran, getting lost in the woods, saved again by the axuli, how he felt worthless and was prepared to die, and his encounter with Rorick and later Tesvi.

"And then after I met Tesvi, we came here and you know the rest."

"Did anything happen on the road? It is a couple of days from Shre to here."

"I mean we went and shared stories with a couple of other travelers at the taverns a couple of nights. One of them offered to take me back to Lagdin. I guess we can both see how that turned out." Alechi let out a slightly uncomfortable chuckle.

"So we can! That is a bigger breakthrough than I believe you are giving yourself credit for. Did Tesvi try and stop you?"

"No. He said it was up to me."

"Then that is indeed a good, no, an amazing step forward for you. Not many would pass up an opportunity to turn home after a journey as harsh as yours. Understand you've done well in making that choice to stay on your journey."

"Thank you?"

"You're welcome. Yes, you are welcome. I do believe my initial assessment was correct. Rorick taught you much about it and it seems my task will be to remind you of who you are in relation to you, your family, your village, us in Som Catre and particularly the axuli."

"I'm not entirely sure what that means."

"That's okay. It will make sense in time. Though I do have another question: why did you ever go out in the first place?"

"I thought I told you it was because I wanted to kill an actusfie?"

"But why did you want to do that?"

Alechi did not respond.

"Think about that question while you are here, and on your journey home. It will certainly aid you." Then he turned his attention to the yet-untouched hourglass that remained on the table between them. It was strange to Alechi the hourglass was there considering the shaman before him had not used it when they first sat down. He thought it merely decorative but as Exsanai's attention turned toward it, Alechi was drawn as well.

"Well," the shaman said, "that will be enough for today."

"I would have thought we would have done more."

What a wast-

"We could, but seeing as there is still some daylight left, I supposed you might want to join the others who were playing in the central courtyard."

"No, I... I couldn't," Alechi protested. "They don't know why I'm here."

"Why would they care? To them, you are another person to play with."

"They don't know me."

"Of course not. Why would they? You haven't introduced yourself yet." The shaman took the few moments of silence that remained after his comment to suggest, "Would you like me to introduce you?"

Alechi turned red as he stood up, "No! I'll introduce myself." He hesitated, drew in a breath, and let it out. "You're sure I'm not too old?"

The shaman smiled, "You're never too old to be a child." The pair left the small room and returned to the courtyard where the children were still playing. Though the orange sky of early evening signaled they would not continue for long.

Alechi stood on the side of the street, simply watching. The old shaman nudged him on the back, "Get in there already. You're losing daylight." A smile spread across Alechi's face and he ran to the young boy who seemed to be giving all the commands and introduced himself.

"Well, hi. I'm Wilrune, but you can call me 'Will,'" said the young boy, no older than Beth. "We are playing our last game right now, but you can join if you wanna. Do you know the rules?" But before Alechi could even draw enough breath to say no, Will, about a foot shorter than Alechi, reached up and pat his shoulder, "You'll figure them out!" And ushered him toward the larger group, introducing him to everyone else. Over on the side, Exsanai let out a short chuckle.

After everyone was gathered into a general area and facing Will, he began to shout commands to the group. Though he was very confused about the roles, he soon found himself miming the actions of those around him. Sometimes Will would call for everyone to run to the right, then the left, then for everyone to be still as a statue. When everyone was still, he would walk between everyone and try to make them laugh by making faces until he felt enough time had elapsed and he gave the word that the others could breathe again. In the first few rounds no one was out. Other times, Will called out different animals. When he said, "Stag!" everyone stood tall and spread their fingers wide, placing them on their heads as though they were antlers. "Horse!" required two people, one pulling the other by their legs. "Bunnies!" required the children to sit in a small group of three on the cobbled stone.

Eventually, some of the other kids got out. Will had been going easy on Alechi and always gave enough time for him to find a group and never bothered him with laughing; however, once it seemed the boy from Lagdin had managed to grasp the game, Will finally got him out.

But in a game such as this, much like Wolf and Sheep, no one was ever truly out. This part of the game Alechi felt he knew well. In addition to aiding Will in making the other kids laugh whenever they were "statues," those who were out waited on the sides, holding the wall of a nearby tailor shop for the long anticipated, "Wolf attack." During such an event, the kids who were still considered in, had to make it to the other side of the courtyard and touch the wall of a sweets store to be considered safe. All others, if touched by someone who was out, would be out. Will enjoyed luring those who were in to the tailor shop's wall, continuously urging them left until they were only a few feet from the wall before calling for a "Wolf attack." The kids would giggle as they approached the tailor shop wall, anticipating needing to run and taking the smallest steps they could toward the wall.

Alechi felt most prepared for the "Wolf attack" after he watched it a couple of times, confused by the instruction at first. After the third attack, he waited in eager anticipation, ready to participate for himself at last.

The children began to approach. Giggles filled the courtyard. Then came the loud cry of Will, "Wolf attack!" All the children that remained, most of whom were young, seemed like easy targets to Alechi. He leapt off the wall and sprinted to one of the little boys. He let out a howl. Then he gripped the arm of the boy, causing him to fall the ground and begin to cry. Another howl broke the air, but murmurs of concern soon overwhelmed them.

Will approached the fallen boy and did his best to make sure he was okay, summoning a few of his friends to help him stand. The boy's mother was nearby and came over to make sure he was okay.

She looked at Alechi distraught and walked sternly toward him. Alechi was ready, he realized now what he had done. He had not meant to hurt the boy, yet the boy was bleeding. His arms and legs were covered in scratches and cuts from the cobbled stones below. Alechi knew he did not want to repeat what he did to Casey, especially with strangers, but he did. Alechi braced himself, but the stern mother's voice never began to speak.

Will had stepped between the mother and Alechi and said simply, "He's new. I'm sure he didn't know."

The mother prepared to formulate a response but gave up and walked her child home.

"Thanks, Will," Alechi said.

"Alechi," Will's vented gravely. "That's not okay-"

"I know..."

Then why did you do it?

"Then don't do it again. You need to learn to play." Will's words pierced him in a way he had not expected.

Already made new enemies I see.

"And," Will began, Alechi flinching in anticipation, "you're welcome to learn with us." He smiled at Alechi and then dismissed everyone as night was fast falling.

"Alechi," the shaman called from behind him, "let's return to the keep for now."

Alechi walked over to his city guide and new mentor. He felt sullen and disappointed in himself, yet most of all confused. Will's words had left him wondering whether he hated him or they were already friends.

"Don't worry," the shaman said. "You'll learn soon enough how you can be a child again. Will is always happy to help."

Alechi smiled at the thought.

Arriving again at the keep, they wove through the hallways to what Alechi assumed to be the backside of the keep. Along the way, Exsanai pointed out a door with steam emitting from it: the bath. When they got to what would be Alechi's room, Exsanai showed him a wardrobe with a few changes of clothes and a towel.

Then Alechi was left to his own.

He went to the baths and, finding them unoccupied, cleaned himself vigorously, sinking deep into the large in-ground basin, inattentive of its depth. Alechi wondered at the question from earlier, why had he wanted to kill an actusfie? Yet, before he could begin to formulate any thoughts he began to feel the weight of sleep on his eyes, the taxation of the day finally seizing him. His mouth began to fill with water. Jolting up in the realization that he did not want to be found drowned in the baths, he dried himself in a rush, leaving wet spots all over his body, and found his room.

"Why?" was all he could ask himself. But before he could form an answer, before the actusfie could induce unnecessary considerations, a lone owl hooted, and sleep overtook him.

13

Forge

As dawn tore through his tinted window, Alechi woke to the sounds of a living city. Already, children were playing in the courtyards, shamans wandering the halls, and the metallic ring of hammer on steel echoed through the city. A series of deep bells tolled high above him from somewhere in the keep.

Alechi dressed in a tunic that was left for him. He had two new options before him, and he chose the short-sleeved, earthy-red tunic; the rest of the clothing was much the same between the options before him. He pulled on one of the pairs of tawny trousers, wrapped a belt around his waist and slipped on the pair of boots that, miraculously, fit comfortably. The clothes were clean and smelled fresh to Alechi. Out of curiosity, he picked up the shirt he had worn the day before for a sniff, instantly regretting it. He tossed it into the corner of his room and out of his mind. He tugged on his shirt and though he had yet to look into a mirror or see any semblance of his reflection, he felt confident and sure of himself for the first time in years.

Exsanai was waiting outside Alechi's door and led him to the dining hall, where he enjoyed a hearty breakfast supplied by generous donations from the people of Som Catre. A variety of meats and nut-covered loaves of bread scented the room with a myriad of smells. While he ate in silence, those sharing his table certainly did not. They spoke joyfully of news they heard from afar and from down the street, recounting experiences and encounters they had with the people. Alechi was the only person in the hall who was not a shaman. Though he was told there were other tourists and visitors from afar who had spent the night, he did not see them. However, it did not matter. The shamans at his table, Exsanai included, made him feel as though he had been there his whole life. Then, the time came for the shamans to report to their duties around the city, aiding the sick, giving food to those in need, repairing homes, and welcoming visitors.

Alechi and Exsanai finished their meal and returned to the room they had been in the day before.

"Now Alechi," the shaman began, settling in, "part of preparing you to face the actusfie inside is aiding you in your control of yourself."

The boy acknowledged the statement with a nod.

"Another will have you doing a job here at the keep, but we will discuss that after you begin your practice with this first bit of training."

"What will I be doing?"

"We will discuss that, as I said, at a later time," The shaman looked at the hourglass that stood still on a small table beside them. The wood that formed its supports was ornately carved with images not only of antlers and stags but of trees, flowers and grasses. There was hardly an inch of it that was not covered in some design. Even the globes had been given a scratched-on design of intersecting, spiraling lines that funneled to the throat of the hourglass.

The two of them stared at the hourglass for a few moments before the trance that had entrapped both of them was broken by the elderly shaman, "Speaking of time..." he said, standing to reach over to the hourglass while Alechi remained seated, a little confused about how he should act. "Yes, speaking of time, that is nearly the subject of this first trial. So sit up straight, that's it, hands on your lap, there you go, and you may want to close your eyes because once I turn this hourglass, you cannot move until the final grain of sand falls to its bottom. If you move, you will have to start over. No talking either. Not to yourself, not even to me. Got it?" The silence answered for him. "Good. Begin." And the hourglass was reversed, and the sand started to trickle down in near complete silence.

Alechi thought he was ready, but now he felt a sudden urge to scratch his nose, yet he resisted it. His body started to itch all over.

What even is the point of this?

In an attempt to dispel the actusfie and the sudden, source-less itch, he squirmed.

The sand stopped falling and Alechi reopened his eyes. The shaman turned the hourglass and the sand that had fallen was being drained back into the other half. While they waited, Exsanai broke the silence.

"You were doing well. What happened?"

"The actusfie and an itch."

"All you must do is ignore them, rejoice that you will be rid of them soon enough. A victory believed will be a victory earned. For now, however, your goal is simply to sit. Now," the sand had finished falling back into a single half, "let's try again. Ready? Begin."

You can't ignore me forever, you know.

The itch began to return, and his head felt as though it was begging him to scratch it.

Why are you even doing this? This does nothing. I am still here!

In his frustration, he forgot his temporary vow of stillness again and stretched the back of his head. The sand stopped falling and the hourglass was reset.

"Remember, this is a temporary test. Moving and scratching is not evil, but if you can forfeit the good, how much stronger you will be against that which is evil. I promise, if you can resist scratching or moving now, you can scratch all you want later. Ready? Begin."

The process continued over a few more attempts, each time Alechi would make it further through the hourglass and soon enough, it was faster for them to wait for the hourglass to finish whenever he squirmed, tapped his foot, hummed or breathed too heavily. The last of which the actusfie found a poor excuse to stop the attempt and Alechi found it to be one as well. "This is ridiculous!" he vented, as the air seemed to pop out of his ears in a mixture of concentration and frustration. "I can't do it!"

"That's enough for today," the shaman said placidly. "I will leave you some advice for the next time. I want you to consider this, I am not asking you to not scratch, not move, not speak, not squirm and all the other hundreds of things you want to do, I am asking you only to do two things: sit still and be quiet. The difficulty may seem like it comes from this simple task, but consider it the other way, that it is the hundreds of things that burden you even now even though the task is easy. Do not make sitting still and being quiet the burden to struggle against, but open yourself to it and let the itches and thoughts fade away. They may be important, but they are not important now. We'll come back to this later. I must attend to my duties at the gate where I found you. I've been granted shorter shifts so that I may help you, but I still must attend to them. In the meantime, how about you join the others by the fountain?"

"What about the other job for me?"

"How strange!" the elderly shaman said, exaggerating his interest and sitting back in his chair. "A boy that wants to work instead of play?"

"I just want to get rid of the actusfie, and you said the job was part of that," Alechi rationalized.

"Well, Alechi, consider joining the other children as part of your job, too," Exsanai chuckled lightly. "There are sometimes more important things than merely ridding yourself of an evil, most of the time it means gaining some great good. Friends are one of these great goods. Go make a few."

Exsanai did not even allow Alechi a chance to respond, but he stood, ushering the boy from the room and toward the main entrance. From there, Alechi assured Exsanai that he knew the way to the fountain and the elderly shaman departed from him with a small smile.

Alechi wandered through the town to where the children had been playing the day before beside the fountain and discovered a smaller group playing today. Will was still among them but was leading a different game today. It was a simple game as they tossed a ball between each other randomly. Whoever dropped the ball, or delivered a short, uncatchable throw, assumed the position to the left of Will. Before each throw, the child had to call out a number and send it to the corresponding child who had to then receive it by echoing their number and calling a new one as they sent the ball flying. If they failed to echo their number when called or sound out a new one, it was as good as a dropped ball. Each child barely held the ball for longer than a moment.

Will noticed Alechi's approach and offered him freely, before the boy could even think of denying the offer, the position at his left. "Alechi, you'll be number thirty-..." he did a quick count, verifying the number of children playing, "one. This one is a little easier to pick up on than the last." The young boy from Som Catre smiled, then shouted, "One-one, fifteen-fifteen!" Will tossed the ball to the child across the circle from him.

"Fifteen-fifteen, four-four!" The boy responded, then threw the ball to a child a few places to Will's right, and so the game continued.

Eventually, Alechi began making his way up to the thirtieth rank as he was reassigned when a girl stumbled and could not think of a new number to call out, assuming the thirty-first position for herself.

The game continued and the ball was reaching Alechi more frequently as he arrived at the twentieth position, making an easy call out, but a more challenging game for him.

"One-one, twenty-twenty!" Will called out at the start of a new round, somehow managing to maintain his position for some time.

Alechi eagerly received the ball and responded, "Twenty-twenty, three-three!" He sent the ball to a child a couple of spaces to Will's right, hoping to get someone in a higher position so he could advance further, but the child caught it and mirrored Alechi's response. He was not ready when the ball came back and he fumbled it to the ground.

That can't be in the rules.

Alechi groaned in frustration, "You can't do that."

"He can, Alechi," Will said.

"That throw was short then," Alechi protested.

Will simply gestured to his left and Alechi tread begrudgingly to the position. He brought the ball with him, handing it to Will so a new round could begin.

"That wasn't fair," Alechi complained as he assumed his position.

"It was as fair to you as your call was fair to him, Alechi," Will whispered. "One-one, three-three!" he shouted, starting the game again, but instead of looking at the child in the third position, he looked to his left, catching the child off-guard. The child dropped it. The round was already over and Alechi had been granted the thirtieth position again. "In this game, you have to be ready at any moment, Alechi." The boy who had been in third picked up the ball and began walking over. Will continued, "And there's no fun complaining about losing because that just means you aren't willing to play again."

The game continued, and Alechi had advanced to the tenth position, falling to the thirty-first a few times but with a better attitude, before the shaman reappeared in the courtyard, beckoning Alechi back to the keep.

"How was the game?" Exsanai asked as they strolled through the streets back to the keep at the center of the three mountains.

Alechi hardly had to think of his response before he blurted it out, unexpectedly even for him, "It was fun!"

The shaman smiled. "I'm happy to hear that."

It was early afternoon when they arrived back at the keep and settled back into the room with the hourglass. The attempts continued for some time.

Alechi shifted his leg as it felt sore from sitting too long and Exsanai once more stopped the trial, allowing the sand to fall the rest of the way down the hourglass' throat. The boy clenched his fists and stomped, releasing a tiny tantrum that had built inside him.

Exsanai opened his mouth to speak, but before he did, he noticed Alechi take a deep breath and mutter something as he exhaled. "What was that?" the shaman asked.

"It's no use complaining," Alechi responded fervently. "Not if I'm willing to try again." The last grain of sand fell to the bottom. "I'm ready," he said. "I just need to focus on the easy part, right?"

Exsanai smiled as he turned the hourglass over for another attempt.

Slowly, the light from the upper window shed its light higher and higher up the door in the otherwise dark room, indicating the falling of the sun. When the light was thin and only a few stray golden beams touched the top of the door, Exsanai announced they were finished for the day.

As the shaman stood to leave the room, Alechi asked, "What about the other job?"

"Ah, yes, a simple question. Would you prefer to help in the garden, fostering the plants of the people or would you like to help in the forges, shoveling coal?"

"That's easy, I used to help with the gardens when I was younger, so I'll do that."

The shaman made an uninterested "hm" and said, "I see." Then he shepherded the boy back to his room for another night.

Alechi engaged in his routine from the night before, bathing and then falling right asleep, eager to help in the garden so he could feel at home once more.

The next morning, Alechi awoke to bells tolling. He put on some day clothes. A mellow, long-sleeve, linen tunic with a brown trim around the neck, perfect for garden work. He exited his room and Exsanai was nowhere to be found.

He felt lost and strangely confused. But as if answering his silent prayer, another shaman approached him. He was a younger shaman yet retained an appropriate air of authority. "May I help you find some place?" he offered.

"I'm supposed to meet with Shaman Exsanai, but I don't know where he is."

"How about we make our way to the main entrance, I'm sure he'll find you there."

Alechi nodded. The two of them shared basic small talk, yet neither shared their name to the other. They passed through a well-kept courtyard of flowers, one that Exsanai likely spoke of. Each flower bloomed differently, a different color, a different shape, some were budding and others were already in full bloom and even some were preparing to wither. Even in the winter, the Shamans found a way to make red, yellow, blue, and pink appear in the garden. Some of the shamans were pouring plenty of water over each plant to aid them as best they could, but even some things in that garden were out of their control. They could nurture, shelter, water, and supply everything, but only the axuli could grow the plants.

Eventually, they arrived in the main hall where Alechi first stepped foot within the light gray stone walls. He now took more time to appreciate the flags he hardly had time to notice the days before. He had always been rushed to the next location and never thought to notice the decorations on the walls.

All the flags had the same symbol of the stag he had seen at the entrance though they differed in the base color and shape. Some were rectangular banners, others dovetailed and some came to a point. Each flag hung high on the walls. Shields bearing the same crest with crossed swords behind them hung a little lower on the walls between well-placed torches to keep light even in the darkest places of the keep. A large circular rug lay in the center of the room and its entirety also bore the same crest. Everywhere he seemed to look, he could see a white stag somewhere in his line of sight.

Simple wax candles, most of which were white, but some were green or bright yellow, were seen everywhere, almost always in pairs. Beneath one prominent image of the stag, directly facing the entrance, was a somewhat strangely alone white candle encased in yellow glass.

The shaman guiding Alechi noticed the traveler's curiosity and smiled. "That is Serinth. One way to think about him is that he is the axuli, the first and the last. He is the one who made all that we know, even the actusfie."

"Why would he do that?" Alechi's question, though tinged with an anger mixed with grief, was out of simple curiosity and his focus was still on the stag.

"All the creatures were created for the good of all, the actusfie were axuli that thought themselves higher than others, than Serinth himself. We all only ever desire good things, or at least some good within a thing. The actusfie use their powers only to destroy rather than protect, manipulate rather than guide. They were particularly jealous of the aid Serinth gave to us when we were lost, even more so when he led us here to Som Catre. Sometimes it can feel like we are more like them; unlike them, however, we choose to learn from our mistakes and use our powers and lives in pursuit of the good we perceive rather than only ever using them to rid ourselves of another."

"Why not just destroy the actusfie then? Since they went against him?"

"It is not desirable for a creator to destroy his creation, especially not when there is still hope for Serinth to bring something good out of everything."

"What if they are hopeless?"

"One is never without hope."

It was then Exsanai revealed himself from the corridor nearby. "Are you ready, Alechi, to resume your training?"

His voice caught the young boy by surprise and broke him free from the trance he had on the stag. He looked to Exsanai and made eye contact and nodded slightly with a quiet, "Yes, sir."

Exsanai once again led them to a private room with an hourglass and sat him down in a chair. "Remember," he began, "let yourself be bored, let yourself do nothing. It is not a matter of restriction or restraint, but a matter of controlling what you want to do in the moment."

"Right. I'm ready," Alechi said, drawing a deep breath as Exsanai turned the hourglass. He reminded himself in his mind, *Let the rest of it fade away, the task is easy.* The time passed slowly as he kept his eyes closed, resting his hands on his lap. The shaman was watching him carefully for any sign of movement. The boy was making steady progress with each attempt.

After a few hours more of practice, Alechi succeeded.

"Congratulations, young man," Exsanai said, a smile spreading across his face. "Remember, this was a mere test of your ability to control yourself. If you can control yourself for ten minutes at a time, you can control yourself as often as you want to. Self-control is an exercise that must be practiced and this is one you can always fall back on, seeing as it doesn't require anything other than yourself."

"I feel better."

"And with a routine established, your control can last throughout your daily life. It is nice to keep busy, but busyness is a distraction, a good start, hardly control."

"Well, then what's next?"

"Your next goal with this form of self-discipline will be an hour," the shaman said nonchalantly. Alechi was fazed but for a moment before he trusted that what the shaman spoke of was possible. "Worry not, young man, I'm not as strict with the hour as I am with the minutes. For now, however, let us make our way to where you will work while here."

Alechi was eager to return to the garden. Its scents drew him closer. He gave a short nod.

The shaman walked him back the way he had come this morning, but he did not stop as they passed through the garden. "We aren't stopping here," he said while the boy hesitated to leave the greenery behind. Alechi had no chance to respond as the shaman continued further into the depths of the keep.

The air grew warm and at the end of the hall, Alechi could see the warm glow of burning coals.

"I thought I was going to work in the garden," the boy said, suddenly stopping in his tracks.

"I said no such thing."

"But I don't know how to do this."

"And that is why you will be far more attentive to it instead of allowing your mind to wander as you garden."

Alechi could think of no counter and instead took a deep breath and pressed forward toward the forges. There he encountered a thick and heavy metal door with a wheel, covered in dirty cloths, to open it. A small, barred window allowed the light and some of the scorching heat to radiate beyond it.

Exsanai motioned for Alechi to turn the wheel and open the door, a silent command which the boy obeyed.

The heat was immense. Already, Alechi was beginning to sweat.

He was used to the southern cold and now he stood but a few feet from an oppressive furnace. All the smoke funneled through a singular, massive chimney in the center of the room. The fires roared and metal clanked so often that it was hard for Alechi to even hear his own thoughts, *But perhaps*, he mouthed to focus the thoughts in his mind, *that is what he wants for me.*

A broad man, tall and muscular, was tending to a metal he held in the furnace. The man suddenly pulled it out and held it against the anvil. He was forging a blade, striking it repeatedly to refine its shape.

"Smith!" Exsanai shouted over the din of the forge. The man looked up and searched the room for the source of the noise before settling his eyes on the boy and the shaman. A few others were in the forge, tending to their own weapons or crafting nails and other fine trinkets, but he paid them no heed.

The smith set the blade he was forging beside the furnace and wiped his hands with a dirty rag. He approached the novel pair and offered his hand to the young boy. Like the shaman, he raised his voice to speak, "Welcome! I'm Smith Kalvil! Have you ever worked in a forge before?"

Alechi shook his head.

"That's alright, you won't be doing anything too difficult! Though you may want to roll up your sleeves, it gets a little warm in here!" He gave the shaman a look as if to ask why he had allowed the boy to wear a long sleeve tunic today.

"I leave him in your care!" the shaman said. "Let him go whenever you feel he has done enough for the day!"

Kalvil nodded then motioned for Alechi to follow him. He brought the boy to a pile of coal with a wide, nearly flat shovel stuck in its center. Alechi stared at the pile. It was near a central furnace that fueled nearly the entire forge. Many of the other workers used the heat from the same furnace, but a few smaller crucibles were scattered throughout the forge.

"After it starts to feel too hot," Kalvil explained, "throw in another shovel!" He patted Alechi on the back and left him on his own. Alechi rolled his sleeves as high as he could, but he could not convince them to stay on his upper arms and they fell back down at awkward times. He picked up the shovel and plunged it into the mass of black coals and forced them into the flames.

14

Claim

Alechi *worked as best he could* in the forge for the remainder of the day. The labor was repetitive and simple. For the boy, it allowed him time, once he had mastered the simple art of shoveling large piles of coals into an already scorching forge, to free his mind.

The engagement of his whole body inhibited the actusfie within Alechi's mind. He found the task itself to remind him much of his time with Rorick and of his time with Exsanai as he learned the exact opposite task of being still for a time.

When the sun set, Kalvil dismissed everyone in the forge. Most returned to their homes to be with, Alechi could only assume, their families. The boy, however, was left to simply turn down the hallway and return to his room.

Alechi washed away the ash and charcoal that blackened his skin with a few small buckets of water. The dark water trickled into a drain on the far side of the baths designated for most of the grime of the day, then he sank into the large pool of water that somehow managed to keep its warmth. Once more he was alone in the baths, and while he wanted to stay longer, he was once again tired enough to desire a mattress over the possibility of drowning.

The next morning came and no one was outside Alechi's door. Looking both ways down the hall, still discovering nobody, he elected to make his way to the dining hall and arrived a few minutes before they would finish serving the food. Exsanai had not shown himself, at least to Alechi's knowledge, at the morning meal and when all the others had dispersed from the hall, Alechi was left alone with no one to lead him anywhere next.

It seems they have forgotten you.

The thought lingered, echoing through his mind as its influence trickled into his very bones. Alechi's resolve then revealed its might and cast the thought from his mind.

They have not forgotten me.

But Alechi thought of little else to do. He could wait in his room and practice sitting for an hour as Exsanai had told him would be his next milestone, but he preferred something more active. The forge, he pondered for a moment, was an option but he thought that if no one had come to gather him for it, he was not needed there at present. *You don't know how to run a forge by yourself after all, do you?* So the final option he considered was to go to the courtyard with the children and join in their games for the day.

Alechi wondered as he wandered to the courtyard what it was they would be playing whenever he arrived. When he arrived, he found a different child was leading the game today, though Will was still present. It was the same game he had played the first day he had joined the group, and they welcomed him readily.

The new leader of the game was as effective as Will when it came to keeping the game fast and fun. Alechi was out soon enough, as was Will, which perplexed Alechi. Will seemed to Alechi to be the master of all the games, *How did he lose so early?*

Will noticed Alechi staring at him as the question, and possible answers, ran through his mind. The leader had yet to call for a wolf attack and there were still about a dozen children playing the proper game. While they waited by the wall, Will spoke, "I think this part of the game is more fun."

He likes losing? He sounds like a f-

But Alechi cut the actusfie off with a question, "Why?"

Will looked to the leader of the game, raised his hand, and, when the leader looked over, gave him a nod. "Wolf attack!"

Alechi was startled for a moment as the call registered with him, he darted toward the mass of children and he was fast enough to easily tag any of them. When the attack finished, Alechi, Will and some of the newly-outs retreated to the wall.

"How many did you get?" Alechi asked. "I got two."

"None."

Alechi was vexed. "You can't be serious. I've seen you run, you're faster than I am."

"But that's not where the fun is."

As the end of the game was approaching, more "wolf attacks" could be expected and Alechi anticipated this by keeping the tips of his finger on the wall while he remained as far from the wall as his arm would allow. "What do you mean by that?" Alechi asked, bouncing to keep his legs ready.

Will smiled at him. "There's more to games than just making sure *you* have fun."

Shortly after, another "wolf attack" was called and everyone darted off the wall again. Alechi led the pack but Will's words echoed from his mind through and to his heart. As he approached the first child so vulnerable and easy to reach, he slowed his pace but emulated an appearance of running. The child giggled as he turned back frequently to look at Alechi, his pursuer. Alechi noticed Will was doing the same, chasing the children to the other wall, but never tagging them. Other children who were out certainly were making an effort to tag those who were still in so a new game could begin, but Alechi felt in his heart a joy he had not known to be possible. Will wore a huge, happy grin on his face as he trailed back to the wall at the end of the attack, and though he did not notice it himself, Alechi wore one as well.

For each of the following "wolf attacks" and all the future rounds of the game, Alechi followed Will's example. It was hardly a challenge for him to catch the children whenever he played the role of "wolf," but he found an irreplaceable joy in the laughter of the others.

At the end of it all, Alechi still found himself out of breath as the sun set, indicating the close of the day and the return of many children to their homes in the city.

"It's a lot more fun, isn't it?" Will said. "Helping others to have fun?"

Alechi stretched his back, recovering from his hunched position and heavy breathing, then spoke through his smile, "Yeah. Thanks for showing me, Will."

Will patted Alechi on the back, "I'm glad you had fun. 'Till next time." Will departed with a wave and Alechi strolled back to the keep.

When Alechi entered the dining hall, he was quickly met by Exsanai and Kalvil. Kalvil's hand reached awkwardly behind his own neck as he cast his gaze downward and Exsanai's stoic expression haunted Alechi.

"Alechi, where were you today?" the shaman asked first.

"We missed ya at the forge," Kalvil said, his speech far more comfortable and sure than his posture.

"I didn't realize I was supposed to go there, I was with the other children playing games."

The shaman stared for a moment then conceded, "I suppose I may not have been the most clear, Alechi. You are to report to the forge daily and I will retrieve you from there when I return from my post at the southern gate. I think we can reasonably assume that you meant no ill by it, especially since I did tell you to consider joining the other children as part of your training, but I must ask you to be more mindful of the task at hand."

"I'm sorry, I didn't realize..."

"Yes, but if you do not know, ask. However, since you did not know, I cannot hold you fully accountable for your absence," Exsanai said.

Kalvil spoke next, "I'll see you tomorrow morning then." He bent over to speak into Alechi's ear, "Sorry kid, the shaman made me come here. Don't be too hard on yourself for this." He patted his shoulder twice then left.

When Kalvil had departed and only Exsanai and Alechi remained, the shaman asked another question, "Did you learn something today?"

"That I should be in the forge until-"

"Not that, I'm sure you won't forget that. It is hard to forget mistakes. You said you were playing games with the other children. Did you learn anything from them? What did you do?"

Alechi recounted his experience playing the game and Will's attitude when it came to the "wolf attacks." The entire time he spoke, the wide grin that gripped his face during the game lingered in every word. "There's just something fun about watching the younger kids have fun."

The shaman smiled and agreed. "Well, let's get you some food."

Alechi felt starved with how much energy he had spent playing with the others and was thankful for the chicken breast served for supper in the dining hall. While they ate, Alechi shared more details of his time during the game, including each time he got out. The shaman listened patiently to Alechi's tale and when the meal had finished, walked with him back to his room.

"Remember, Alechi," the shaman spoke, "be at the forge tomorrow. Rest assured, I'll be sure to allow you some time to play with the others, but there is more to do than play."

"Thank you, Shaman Exsanai," Alechi answered.

Alechi completed his nightly routine of bathing, a luxury he was happily taking advantage of, and fell asleep.

The next morning, Alechi donned the same clothes he had worn the day before, finding the other clothing in desperate need of a wash. He ate breakfast then navigated to the forge where the roar of flames and clanging of metal awaited him. Even as he approached the glowing light at the end of the hall, he could feel the heat pouring out of the forge.

Alone as he approached the door, he took the time to suck in a deep breath in preparation for the blast of heat he knew he would feel the moment he cranked the door free of its hinge.

Kalvil was dumping pile after pile of coals into the furnace as if he wanted it to be extra hot, and when he noticed Alechi, he had the boy take over the shoveling of coals.

"I need the forge kept high today, at least for the beginning!" Kalvil shouted over the roar of the furnace. "Just keep shoveling until I say so!"

Alechi stood motionless for a moment as his thoughts gathered. *Is this punishment for missing yesterday? I thought he did not mind.*

He is here to punish you. The shaman is just the same. This is torture, is it n–

The thought was again silenced as the shovel was pushed into Alechi's grip and he was essentially walked over to the bright furnace in the midst of a mostly dark forge. Kalvil gave him a nod, then left to resume his own work.

Alechi wiped the sweat that had already formed on his forehead despite his fresh exposure to the forge and began shoveling. Last time, he would throw in a shovel or two of coals whenever Kalvil asked or he had noticed the furnace cooling himself, but the task he had before him was different. It was a consistent, repetitive task. *Plunge, lift, toss. Plunge, lift, toss. Plunge, lift, toss.* The mantra formed in Alechi's mind kept it occupied and, more critically, tranquil. The actusfie found no way in, even in such a simple task, Alechi's mind was devoted fully to it.

The entire morning passed and Kalvil told Alechi he could take a break as the metal he was working with for the day had already melted and was in its stone cast, waiting to be refined later. Alechi cooled himself off by taking a short walk to the baths to rinse his face and returned to find Shaman Exsanai ready for him.

"It seems we had just missed each other, but there you are," the shaman said. "Come, the time has come for you to practice being still for an hour." The shaman ushered Alechi from the room as the boy waved goodbye to the smith, unsure if he wanted to begin the shaman's new task. "I'll give you a choice, though I warn you one is more difficult than the other: would you prefer to practice in the room where we practiced before or in the garden?"

Alechi's heart skipped a beat as he answered instantaneously, "The garden."

The shaman smiled, "So it shall be. It is the harder choice, though it does better prepare you for what is to come."

Alechi barely heard the statement and thought little of it, he had longed to spend time in the garden, and was finally afforded the chance. That was all that filled his mind.

The shaman quickly set Alechi down, having him sit not on one of the few stone benches in the midst of the garden, but on the grass, surrounded by flowers. There was no hourglass in his midst.

"You are welcome to assume any posture you like, but know that whichever you use, you must not change from it."

"So I can lie down?"

"If you wish."

Alechi reclined onto the grass, stretching his legs and basking in the light of the sun.

"Now much like how I expect you to be at the forge in the mornings without retrieving you, I cannot watch you for the whole hour. Or rather there are other things I must attend to, nor do I want to watch you lie in the grass for an hour, so I will be relying on your word that you have not moved. I will be back every so often to check on you and you have permission to speak so long as you do not move too much. Understood."

Alechi nestled his hands under his head and echoed, "Understood."

Exsanai departed. He returned in increasingly lengthy intervals as he passed to another duty somewhere within the keep to check on the boy.

Alechi had found that as he practiced his stillness, he needed a different position in order to maintain it. He could not lie on his back and sleep because he would try too often to twist to his side. Sitting upright was hard to do while remaining still and the earth, though he thought it soft at first, grew firmer the longer he remained unmoved. Alechi expressed his concerns to the shaman as he passed through.

"Have you considered lying on your stomach with your hands to cushion your face?" the shaman asked.

Alechi did not even bother responding vocally, but simply adjusted to the position. Exsanai was right that this position was the most comfortable for him that he had tried, but Alechi worried as he found himself unable to watch the sun for the time and he felt vulnerable to the environment. He could not crane his neck. His hands were locked underneath his forehead and he had nothing to look at but his hands and the grass beneath him.

When Exsanai next returned, it was a half hour later and Alechi was still in his position, unmoved, but he was restless. The shaman sensed this in him and told him he had gotten far enough in the day and could go to the courtyard with the other children.

Thus the pattern continued for a month. Alechi went in the mornings to the forge, fueling the flames, his mind fading into a mantra with the crackle of coal and the ring of hammer on metal. Kalvil guided the boy in sharpening and polishing of swords and by the end of the month had Alechi forging nails, familiarizing him with metal. Next, he would practice remaining still in the garden, and it took him only two weeks to reach the full hour, but it was unbeknownst to him as Exsanai had simply left the boy undisturbed as long as he allowed. The time faded and became one that he looked forward to as much as the games he played with the other children. The garden offered Alechi a sense of peace like when the axuli had crawled into his arms. It was as if the gardened welcomed the spirit.

After he had finished his time of stillness, Exsanai encouraged Alechi to join the children at play, and he found himself leading a few games on occasion, growing closer and more familiar with those he met.

Spring was approaching, and though it had not been particularly cold in the region, Alechi felt the spring air warm him as he lay prostrate on the grass.

"Have you moved?" Exsanai asked.

"Only to speak to you," Alechi responded, remaining still.

"You've been here nearly two hours," Exsanai said. "I think you are ready for your next step."

"Which is?"

"If my memory serves me, one of our shamans spoke to you about Serinth, correct?"

Alechi finally rose from his position and gave a simple nod to the shaman.

"Well, your next, and far more important task, is to speak and listen to him."

"I thought the axuli couldn't speak."

"Serinth is no ordinary axuli, he is the creator, he can do whatsoever he wills, though you may not find his voice as distinct as either one of ours." The shaman led him to a simple stone bench in the middle of the garden and welcomed him to sit on it.

"Now," the shaman said, "that rabbit from the night of the wolves, you remember it?"

"How could I not? It saved me."

"Saved you indeed, by sacrificing itself. That axuli acted like few others have. The only other axuli known to lay its life down for another as you described is Serinth himself. Since his sacrifice, no actusfie dared approach this city. Yet he was not destroyed, he was seen only a few days after his sacrifice, wounds and all, before fading into the wind. In our hearts, he made it as clear as the day is bright that he would continue to watch over us in his own spiritual form."

"The axuli have spiritual forms too? I thought that was just the actusfie."

"Where do you think the actusfie got it from? Either way, the rabbit you described was likely Serinth himself once more. The axuli are ordered to protect, provide, aid, and heal. They are more fierce than you can imagine despite their appearances, but only Serinth sacrifices. Remember Serinth is no ordinary axuli, he is greater. Beyond comparison. You've met Serinth before. He guards this city and he guards you personally as well. Others have experienced Serinth's sacrifice as well, as I said, you are far from the first to come here for help-"

You were not spec-

"But do not let that diminish the value of that sacrifice. He has done it for all, he has done it for you, and he will do it for you again if it was ever needed."

"So then how do I reach him again?"

"The same way he guards over you, with your spirit. Use your mind, the very thing that actusfie seeks to corrupt, use your self-control, don't be distracted by the itches or lies the actusfie provides you as it attempted just now. These practices are almost one in the same, self-control will help you reach out with your own spirit starting with your mind."

"I'm not sure I get it."

"Clear your mind as you have been doing when lying here in the garden."

Alechi closed his eyes and took intentional breaths.

"Now what?"

"When you worked in the forge, what did you do? How did you learn your task there? It was through repetition, was it not? This is much of the same."

"How so?"

"Practice focusing your senses on Serinth even if you cannot see him. He will find you."

15

Searching

The weather was warm but not overbearing as the sun shone over them amidst a bright blue sky. The sun itself remained hidden behind the clouds, and the shade from them allowed the breezes that passed through the garden to refresh Alechi as he closed his eyes. He took a few breaths as he held the name Serinth in his mind. The wind rushed through the branches of some of the trees within the garden, rustling the leaves, birds chirped from above him, yet he still did not hear Serinth speak to him.

As if he knew what he was thinking, Exsanai said to him, "Do not give in quite yet, Serinth is listening, listen in return."

Alechi returned his focus to Serinth and said quietly, "I am listening, Serinth." No words on the wind found their way into his ears. Though he recognized the sounds of winds, birds, and city chatter, no heard no clear words. But then, the sun broke through the clouds and shone on the boy in the garden and he felt in his heart a thought that was quiet and soothing, contrasting once more the harsh and loud words he felt when the actusfie spoke.

The thought urged him simply, *Come to me.*

"Where are you?"

Where you need me.

He looked around for any sign of the white stag that had supposedly been speaking to him, and he saw nothing. But the light from the sun was truly blindingly bright. He shielded his eyes and looked up at one of the peaks of the mountains where the sun stood in the sky. The clouds moved in front of the sun once more and Alechi was able to relax his eyes a little. Through the clouds that shadowed the entire land, a new ray of light cast itself somewhere on the forest to the west that was not visible through the walls of the keep and the mountains.

No other words came to him, and though he thought Serinth was gone from his mind, the axuli lingered in his heart and he felt that where the sun shone was where he must go.

"Why do I have to go there if he is here?" Alechi gestured to the forest.

"Why did you have to come here if he was also where you were?" Exsanai proposed. "Sometimes it is not about where you are physically, but where the journey will take you spiritually. Now, just because Serinth calls you to that forest, he does not promise it will be free of danger. Bring your sword and buckler, and even your father's knife, but do not draw them unless Serinth tells you to. Trust in his protection. All is within his command."

Alechi was led back to his room and strapped his weaponry to his belt. He carried the buckler on his arm, the small, round protector ready to face anything that lay ahead of him. He strapped the knife to his right side and the sword on his left, both ready to be drawn if needed, but sleeping in their scabbards until awoken for battle.

"Have everything?"

Alechi nodded.

"Then I shall escort you to the western gate. There a tunnel will lead you into the forest."

"You are not coming with me?"

"If you do not learn for yourself how you are to live, you will never truly understand how you can. I will pray to Serinth that he keep watch over you, but you must start learning to obey Serinth and trust him without my help. I will not be able to watch over you every second of your life, no man can. Serinth will always be there to help you. Others will continue to help you in life. Accept their help, ask for it even, but you must be ready for when others cannot help you. When only you are needed. This is one of those cases. Serinth does not need me in the forest right now. You may want me there so you do not have to claim responsibility if something goes wrong, but that will not help you learn to live and trust his words."

And so Alechi contemplated the shaman's words as they walked in silence through the otherwise buzzing city. For the first time in what felt like years, he could feel the full burden weighing on his heart, no longer masking as something lighter or non-existent by the actusfie. The city was helping him realize that. There was beauty everywhere. The faces of the mountains that looked into the city, carefully guarding over it, were littered with life of all kinds. Each mountain stood in its own majesty and the light touched each one so that none of them reflected the same beauty. The mountain they were walking to was bathed fully in light and the snowy peak radiated blinding light back to the earth and though it was rocky, it bore tall trees and small, yet noticeable flamboyant flowers.

Soon, they approached the tunnel and it was now closer to midday. The clouds had parted slightly but the mountains' breezes kept the warm sun from being overbearing. Here, much like the southern gate Alechi had come to with Tesvi, there were guards and a barracks station to provide a rotation of relief. It was not nearly as busy as the southern gate, the area seemed otherwise deserted. Most of the guards were in the barracks lazing in its shady interior while two would stand by the gate at the ready, supporting themselves with spears, with eyes peering into the well torchlit tunnel awaiting any arrivals.

One of the guards heard the footsteps of the approaching pair, as it seemed this part of the city was quiet enough that only the distant din of the city's hub could overpower the sound of the breeze. The guard looked at Alechi from over his shoulder, used the butt of his spear to lightly tap the other guard's foot and gave him a nod as well. They moved to the ends of the gate, now facing each other instead of the tunnel, making way for the boy far from his home.

"May Serinth protect you, Alechi, and keep you safe from whatever perils you may face along your way," Exsanai said, stopping at the tunnel's arching entrance. The tunnel sloped down and the light from the other side could not be seen.

"Thank you, Shaman."

"Shaman," one of the guards interjected, bowing his head slightly when Exsanai turned to him, "it is rare to see you not at the southern gate, may we have your blessing as well?"

Amused, Exsanai nodded and putting his hands together and spreading his fingers wide, he said simply, "Of course. We thank you, Serinth, for your many blessings upon this city. We ask now that you protect the guards here at this station, that they may complete their jobs with vigilance. May the axuli watch over them and aid them in all their troubles." Then, keeping his hands together, he gestured with them to the two guards and to the barracks. "Go in the light of Serinth."

"Thank you."

"You're welcome, now do let me know when he returns,"

Exsanai said, indicating Alechi. "I'll be in the shamans' keep."

The guards nodded to Exsanai and resumed their vigilant stance on either side of the tunnel. The shaman turned to started to walk away, and after forty paces or so made a turn that removed him from sight. Alechi kept looking back to where Exsanai was, hoping silently in his heart that he would come back. He was nervous to be alone again.

Then, after a few deep breaths, as if summoned by his fears, he felt the actusfie reviving itself within him.

But the feeling subsided.

A sparrow landed on the cobblestone next to him, turning its head side to side, examining its surroundings and hopping short distances. Its hops brought it ever closer to the entrance of the tunnel and there it stopped and looked at Alechi, still paralyzed in place between the guards. The bird then took flight, flying right by the boy's right ear circled in the sky and landed right back where it started. The breath of quiet wind that roared within Alechi's ear seemed to wake him from his paralysis and he now looked at the bird. It leapt once more off the ground and flew a short distance into the tunnel, still within Alechi's sight.

Alechi was fascinated with the behavior of the sparrow, recognizing it now as an axuli; and the guards, who had seen or experienced the wonder on their own journeys, smiled at his recognition.

Alechi lifted his head and grabbed the straps that held his limited gear, and with a sharp exhale, he stepped into the tunnel.

Once he was inside the tunnel, it did not seem so dark. Plenty of sunlight spilled into the shady cave and the torches supplied light. He knew this was the way to Serinth. The axuli that entered the tunnel continued to make short flights every time he caught up to it going deeper into the tunnel yet never out of sight. The damp tunnel walls were cool, and Alechi was soon rubbing his arms for warmth. The cobble from the streets above continued through the way down and the slope was long and shallow.

He walked for about an hour before he finally saw sunlight on the floor of the tunnel ahead of him. Running for the clearing and for warmth, he found the tunnel opened into a vast, vibrant, verdant forest. Though it was all green, the sunlight and the shadows painted various tones that left any traveler breathless at its sight. The tall trees were spread apart wide and their massive moss covered trunks helped the entire setting to appear in unison.

The axuli fluttered up to a tree and called for Alechi's attention with a light whistle. He continued to follow the axuli and each of its beckonings to another tree. The path he tread was level and soft making it easy on his feet as he traveled without ever looking down to where he was walking. He kept his eyes focused on the axuli as it led him through a well-trod path in the forest.

Eventually, the pair found themselves in an open meadow. It reminded Alechi of the glade in which he had encountered his first axuli. Bathed in light, the luscious meadow thrived with life. The sound of a brook could be heard nearby, though he was not sure where it was. Plenty of birds sang their songs, and squirrels and rabbits rustled among the leaves and bushes of the forest. The air felt warm against his skin and even with the bright sun above, he felt nothing but peace and comfort as he stared into the shining meadow before him. He was fully prepared to continue venturing deeper into the forest, but the axuli did not find a new branch. Instead, it landed in the meadow just a few feet from Alechi and bowed its small head as low as it could.

Alechi now stepped past the tree line into the meadow.

Come no further.

Alechi stopped in his tracks. The voice he heard was not his own, nor was it the actusfie's and it was undeniably, yet paradoxically, both from within and without.

Wait here.

The boy fell to the ground and assumed his prostrate position with which he had maintained his hours of silence, expecting that this is exactly what Exsanai had been training him for.

The time passed without a thought that was not his own. Something stirred to his side.

What is that? You should run. Who knows what-

Yet Alechi remained firm and unmoving, casting the thoughts of the actusfie aside. He did not know why, but he felt he could trust the command to wait.

A large stag entered the meadow opposite him, staring confidently at him. Its antlers were tall and branched in a perfect mirror of the other. Its coat was as white and pure as the snowcaps around Som Catre, unstained by mud or leaf. Undisturbed by that which remains below it. Each step the stag took was filled with confidence. It held its head high as it stared straight at the boy. All the noise, including the brook, fell silent. Alechi had yet to see the stag for himself, but remained unmoving, waiting for Serinth. Then, as if it had reached some invisible line, the stag stopped. Alechi felt the stag peering into his mind, his heart, his soul. Alechi could hear his own heartbeat, and though it was fast when the stag first appeared, he found it slowing as he realized who stood before him.

"Serinth," he said. The name came out before he could think it. The stag lowered its antlers and, though Alechi felt nothing pierce him, touched the boy's heart, beckoning him to rise. Alechi stood up and the stag raised its head. In the fullness of Serinth's radiance, he stood momentarily paralyzed. The boy stretched out his hand and touched the muzzle of the stag. His hand graced Serinth's hair, or perhaps it was the other way around.

After he removed his hand, a bright, iridescent light began to radiate from the stag that nearly blinded Alechi had he not shielded his eyes. The dazzling, color-filled glare that stretched out of Serinth's transformation made all other colors pale in comparison. It was the most marvelous thing that Alechi had not quite seen, and it filled his heart with fear, love, and hope if such complex emotions could ever mingle.

Now before him was a rabbit in the place of the stag. It took him a moment to recognize the rabbit as the same one that had followed him from the village, the same patterns of brown fur were on its back and most noticeably to Alechi, the detail that only that rabbit or axuli could have, were the bite marks and fang holes on its neck from when it had rescued him beside the forest stream. The marks from before he met Rorick.

Alechi fell to his knees and held out his hand once more. He felt his chest tighten and a lump form in his throat as he tried to prevent himself from crying, but the rabbit moved its neck to Alechi's hand and, in doing so, allowed him to feel the depth of the holes. No rabbit could survive that, he was sure that the rabbit died. *Death cannot part us*, the words filled his heavy heart and tipped the scales in his mind.

He wept.

I died for you and I would do it again. Take me back with you to Som Catre and present me to Exsanai along with your sword and buckler. He will advise you on what to do. Again, though no words broke the still air, they rooted themselves firmly within his heart. The rabbit leapt into his arms, and Alechi felt once more the warmth of the hearth in his home on a winter day. The comfort brought him peace, and though he still cried, he did it while at peace with the tears, no longer trying to fight them.

The axuli in the form of a sparrow lifted its head and the sound of the forest resumed around them. It moved in front of Alechi, once more beckoning for him to follow. Serinth had made his mind clear enough to follow without hesitation. He was led back through the forest and to the tunnel.

Alechi walked up through the cool tunnel, stifling the sniffles that remained after tears. He saw the guards. They were different from the ones he saw before he entered the forest, and in an effort to save face, he straightened his back. He had made it. The sun was beginning to set on the western horizon behind them and the city began to cool down. But the body of the rabbit and the warmth in Alechi's veins prevented him from even considering a shiver in the tunnel. Once Alechi had stepped onto the main road within the city, one of the guards from before, who had been waiting in the barracks nearby, accompanied him back to the keep.

When they finally arrived back at the keep, the sun had sunken fully below the horizon of the mountaintop but the light still bled over the edge of the earth to leave a lingering cool gray in the sky as night began settling. Exsanai was waiting for them in the foyer of the keep that was littered with the flags and banners of the antlers.

"Well done," he said. He nodded to the guard and the guard turned to return to his post.

"Thank you," Alechi responded. He could not help but smile as the creator was in his arms and it filled him with such joy. "Do you know what's next?"

"I do. Come with me." He turned to enter the room next to the antlers with the yellow candle. The room was the largest in the entire area and it made Alechi wonder how all the other hallways and rooms fit in the keep. "This is the sanctum," Exsanai said plainly. There were columns that supported high arches and vaulted ceilings. Between the columns were rows of pillows for people to sit. There were a few people inside already all facing the same direction as they knelt or sat on the pillows. Ahead was a large altar with another set of antlers behind it. Tall candles were lit on each corner of the altar and high windows let what little light remained inside. It was dark, but not impossible to see.

They approached the dais before the altar, and Exsanai made a deep bow before stepping up to the altar. Alechi waited where he was, but when the shaman looked back to him, he too bowed and made his way up the steps.

"Place the offering here," Exsanai said, hovering his hand over the center of the altar.

Alechi looked at the shaman, who, in turn, indicated at Serinth in his arms. "What are you planning on doing with him?"

But before the shaman could answer the rabbit leapt from Alechi's arms and lay itself down on the altar as it had when it saved him from the wolves.

"And now place your sword and buckler beside him."

Alechi obeyed. Curious, but not questioning.

"Almighty Serinth, willingly offers himself for your protection, for your aid, and your salvation. In offering himself, he unites himself to you and you in turn to the whole of his creation. He reminds you of your own identity as his, as your parents', all of us here, and all who have gone before us into his care."

Exsanai took Serinth, had a brief, quiet dialogue with him then lay him back down. He took out an ornate dagger and raised it high. Distraught, Alechi moved to stop him, but the shaman held up a hand. "Fear not," Exsanai said. "It is his will that this be done."

"But why? He's done enough for me already!"

"He is only doing what he has done before."

The shaman plunged the dagger into the rabbit's neck.

"No!" Alechi still could not understand.

The blood poured out steadily but not in excess. "With the blood of Serinth, may your weapons serve you in protecting yourself from and slaying the actusfie within you." The sword and the buckler were drawn through the blood and wiped clean with a rag. Then Exsanai handed the weapons back to Alechi who stared at them in awe, guilt, and appreciation. Nothing looked different. The weapons still weighed the same. But Alechi could tell, *something* had changed.

Then the shaman cleaned the altar, setting Serinth aside as he did. When he finished, he took Alechi and pointed to Serinth, so the boy would carry him, and they went further into the large sanctum where a fire was burning, maintained by a pair of shaman. This pair of shaman saw the sacrifice on the altar and how the boy and the elder drew near, so they prepared an iron grill to go over the flames, a washing bowl and various tools for preparing the rabbit. Together, the three shamans prepared the rabbit for consumption, removing the hairs and cooking it over the fire. The gamey scent filled the air and reminded Alechi of all the times he had eaten a rabbit while in Lagdin, which was nearly every day. Tears formed in his eyes.

"Each time you brought a rabbit to your shaman in Lagdin, he was asking it for its sacrifice." Exsanai said, sensing Alechi's quiet questions. He continued to work. "Each is an axuli, each is then consecrated to be Serinth to be food to protect you. It was his decision to feed and protect us in such an ordinary manner. The real reason that actusfie has not already taken your whole life is because compared to Serinth who dwells in you through the consuming of his own flesh in the form of the rabbit, that actusfie can do nothing."

Soon, Serinth's flesh was fully prepared. Exsanai took it, tore a piece of its flesh, and offered to Alechi with the words, "Serinth conquers. May your body become more like his, Good, One, and True."

Alechi ate the body of Serinth as did the others with him.

The shamans sat in silence after they ate, quietly offering thanks for the gift they had received in participating in the sacrifice. After some time, however, Exsanai looked to Alechi and led them out of the sanctum.

"Hold tight to Serinth, he will protect you. He dwells within you as he has yet now you have a fuller knowledge of it. You see how he unites us all to one another and defines who we are. He grants you safety, peace and protection, but does not keep you free from strife as it helps you grow closer to him. The decision is now in your hands to release the actusfie from yourself and slay it with the power granted to you by the blade and buckler Serinth has bathed with his own blood."

The shaman handed him the bones, burned clean of any meat on them. "Take these to Kalvil with your sword and buckler, it will be your final task here."

Before Alechi could even realize where he was walking, he was in the forge, face to face with the smith whom he had helped and who had helped him over the last month.

"Shaman Exsanai said you would help me with these," Alechi said, offering the bones.

"Aye, we have a long night. Keep the forge warm. I've made a number of these. And now, you must do your part."

It seemed only the two of them were in the forge. Kalvil instructed Alechi through a process that was foreign and strange to the boy. First, the bones were crushed into a fine powder. Then, the blade of Alechi's sword was melted completely and the powder mixed in with the molten metal. They poured the alloy into a new cast, folding and hammering the metal to keep it strong. By the end of the night, a new sword was forged for Alechi, sharpened and polished. It was no longer mere iron, but blessed steel.

"That's a beautiful sword, Alechi," Kalvil said. "It will serve you well. Well done."

"But what's really different?"

Exsanai, having heard grindstone cease, entered the forge. "You'll find the answer to that in time. Come, let's get you ready," he said, guiding Alechi back to his room. While they walked, the shaman spoke, "You must now return home. Continue to master yourself so you can give it all to Serinth. It is by his power that the actusfie will be slain, not by your own, remember that, but only you can let the evil spirit go, Serinth will not take it from you. Much like the task of controlling yourself, remember this, Serinth asks only two things: treat all with love and rely on him. All else can fade away. You know what helps you, yes?"

"Focusing on Serinth, helping others, and well, others helping me, too."

"A fulfillment of those asks. And what enables the actusfie?"

"Idleness, entertaining despair, loneliness, fear."

"And hundreds of other things, but they can all fade. And are those all good emotions?"

"Yes, as long as I keep them honest." Alechi's answers did not feel as though they came from him, but from Serinth himself.

"Then you are ready to battle the falsehood of an actusfie with the truth of Serinth. Go in his light."

16

The Final Bite

The shamans in the keep helped Alechi prepare for the road home. He was allowed to keep the tunic they supplied him for while he stayed with them. They gave him a new pack full of dried foods, a skin full of water, new blankets that were rolled up and strapped to the bottom of the pack, and a heavy cloak to shield him from any rain or lingering cold.

Exsanai gave him one last instruction, "Ask for all the help you can to complete the ritual. The sooner the better. Your shaman will know what to do."

Alechi nodded. He was now fully equipped for the journey home to Lagdin, but he had one last thing he wanted to do. Alechi requested to be taken to Tesvi's store at the very least to see him again and thank him for his help. A guard was ordered to lead him to the merchant's store.

Tesvi was waiting by the entrance of his store, trying to invite people in as he called out what he had in stock. He caught sight of Alechi and while the boy was still a long way off, Tesvi grew excited, called his name over the crowd and ran to him amidst all the mayhem of the merchants' street, leaving one of his assistants in charge.

"Alechi! It is so good to see you!"

"You too, Tesvi." He was excited but his voice was dry and somber. Tesvi noticed the quaver and welcomed him into the shop to an upper floor where the din of the streets was dim.

Alechi recounted all that happened since their separation at the gate, the truth about the actusfie latched to him, and his encounters with the axuli. "And now," he said, "I'm on my way home. I'm ready now, Serinth made me ready. It feels almost like a thin sheet wrapped around my body ready to fall off and I just need to let it go."

Tesvi was surprised, "I had a suspicion, or two... but I'm glad I was able to get you here! A noble cause indeed." He chuckled as he recalled the mercenaries' tales in the taverns they heard along the way and their own noble causes. An idea then flashed into the merchant's mind, and he looked at Alechi with a gleaming determination that could brighten and encourage even the soul of darkness itself, "I'll take you home."

Alechi tried to stop him, "Tesvi, I can't let you do that! You've done enough just getting me here, it gave me a chance to think and, well, to be without much other worry. You gave me a chance to choose and that is enough. You only just came back to Som Catre and Lagdin is such a long way away."

"It is for that reason that I'm going to take you home," he replied, then mocking one of the mercenaries they had heard he said gruffly, "It is my duty!"

"I'm not going to be able to stop you, am I?"

"Unfortunately not, my good friend. This is the smallest good deed I will ever do with the greatest impact I will ever have in my life. I'm doing this because I want to help you anyway I can. Besides, you're providing free protection right?"

"But how will you get back?"

"I'll figure that out later," Tesvi said as he clapped his hands together in his decisiveness. "Give me a moment to let my assistant know and we'll be off soon enough. Feel free to wait up here."

Alechi made a start to protest but Tesvi had already descended the stairs before he had a chance to voice a syllable. He scanned the room as he waited and saw an oil painting of three people. The tall man on the left was a younger Tesvi wearing a red cap and a fine, dark blue tunic underneath a white mantle with a golden trim. He had his arm behind a woman on his right, her hair was blonde and her eyes were green. Her pale skin and soft face radiated beauty as she managed a smile. She wore a long, flower-embroidered, light blue dress with frills as the skirt fell to the ground. The two adults had their spare hands on the third figure beneath them, a young boy, wearing a tunic that matched Tesvi and a high white collar on his inner shirt. He continued to admire the painting for some time.

Tesvi climbed the staircase and noticed Alechi's enthrallment with the portrait. He stood at the top step and smiled at the appreciation. "They're the reason I help others. They were my real treasures."

The boy returning home stood and stared in reverent silence as his heart sank for his friend.

"Come," Tesvi said, breaking the silence, "we have a long road ahead of us and the sooner we get going, the sooner we will get there."

Alechi nodded in understanding and followed the merchant downstairs and onto the street to a nearby stable that kept the merchant's horses and wagon. They loaded it up with enough of Tesvi's treasures to make trades in the villages they would pass through on their way to Lagdin so the journey could be justified to Tesvi's assistant. Alechi sat with the widower in the driver's seat as he drove the horses through the city and back out the southern gate.

Some time passed along their road to Lagdin. Their visits to the towns and villages along the way were kept brief for the sake of moving along the road. They came to Shre where they had first met, yet the one who introduced them, Rorick, was nowhere to be seen. The sun was setting on Shre, so Tesvi elected they spend the night in Shre.

"Just about another day or so on the road and we will reach Lagdin," Tesvi said, examining a map carefully. "It will be the furthest south I've ever been."

"It's nice there," Alechi said, half-smiling as he unloaded his equipment from the wagon as they made their way to the doors of the tavern. "I can't wait to see it again. Som Catre was beautiful, but there really is nothing like the silence of the forest. There really is nothing like my family. Like my friends."

Tesvi fell silent for a few solemn moments. "They really are hard to replace."

Alechi felt his heart sink with Tesvi's when he recalled the painting in the upper room of Tesvi's store. "Right, I'm sorry."

"It's okay, they are where they belong. Serinth holds them now." Silence settled between them as they made their way to their rooms.

Then the merchant sought to break the silence, bringing to the forefront of his mind a question he had always wondered about the smaller villages. "You've never worried about attacks from the actusfie?"

"I haven't. Our shaman and our guards do a good job protecting us, I had to go out of my way to get into the trouble I'm in."

"I see." He shrugged. "Well, good night, Alechi."

"Good night, Tesvi. And thank you."

Tesvi nodded in response.

The pair settled into their separate rooms for the night. Each room was as small as it was cheap and did not serve as a place for an extended stay. Alechi lay his head down and prepared himself to sleep.

Are you sure you're ready?

He tried to ignore it and shut the actusfie out of his mind. It came back.

You? A kid from nowhere think you can beat me? Why because you think that shiny new sword will protect you? Nothing has really changed. You have always eaten rabbit. That sword is just iron and bone, it cannot kill me any more than it could before. You AREN'T ready.

In a moment of clarity, while the panic neared his heart and he turned uncomfortably trying to dispel the actusfie, he calmed himself and said simply, "I'll never be ready. But if I don't get rid of you now, when will I?"

You will never be ready! I will always be stronger, I will always be better than you!

"Yet you fear the axuli, you fear Serinth. You fear those I rely on, I don't need to be better than you. Now be quiet, I need to sleep."

I cannot be destroyed by you, I am a part of you.

"You can be and you never were." And the actusfie fell silent long enough for Alechi to drift into sleep.

When he awoke the next morning, they cleaned themselves, ate, and packed up eagerly resuming the last leg of their journey. The roads between Shre and Lagdin were where most merchants drew the line for their own safety and where mercenaries demanded higher pay for the protection they provide. Tesvi, however, seemed confident in Alechi's abilities and they set out along the road.

Alechi was hardly familiar with this part of the road, especially considering he abandoned it during his journey north to Som Catre. His eyes turned back and forth to either side as the canopy of diverse trees loomed over the road, hiding whatever dwelled within the dense landscape behind them. Rorick had led him through the woods last time along a direct path from his hut within the woods.

They would have to spend at least one night on the road, there was no way to avoid it. Even as they travelled during the daytime, creatures could be heard stalking them from the shade. When night fell, they set up what they could to defend themselves and started a fire to keep the area from being too dark and too cold.

A twig snapped.

You... the voice inside seemed to taunt him, *may want to run...* it almost seemed to be laughing.

But the actusfie's words of warning backfired from the cowardice they were intended to instill. Alechi rose to his feet and gripped the sword he had yet to use tightly in his hand, holding the buckler in the other. His eyes scanned the tree line and he listened beyond the cackling flames and popping wood to trace the sounds.

A ferocious growl led a large black cougar with glowing eyes that seemed to reflect the firelight out of the woods. It started to pace. Then it struck. The boy narrowly avoided the cougar's first pounce, but it rebounded back onto him. Tesvi awoke from the noise and ran to the wagon to see if he could find a weapon. There was no need for words in such an emergency.

The cougar's jaws opened wide as it kept its weight on the boy's chest, leaning in for a bite. It growled again, but Alechi sent a fist into it. The growl stopped for a moment but ultimately only made the actusfie more agitated. The cougar had kept a paw on his sword arm and seemed to be pressing down even harder on him now as it growled again to go for another bite. Alechi caught the bite with his buckler, stopping the cougar's mouth from closing. The buckler did not crumble. The fangs were mere inches from his forearm as he struggled to keep the buckler in its mouth.

Serinth... Serinth, help me. "Serinth!" the boy cried out.

Only then did Tesvi find Alechi's dagger still strapped to a belt near the campfire. He threw the dagger at the cougar, and it thudded into its side. It let out a yowl as it began to bleed. Alechi was able to push out from underneath it, pin the beast down and thrust the sword into it. The blade did not reach deep before it fizzled into a pile of ash and dust.

"Thank you, Tesvi."

Tesvi smiled. "No need to thank me, Alechi. We did not kill that thing."

March was helping his father chop some firewood. The burden of keeping the homes warm was long gone and spring was coming into its fullness. The freezing nights of winter were behind them and the days would only continue to get warmer but never excessive. He swung the ax hard, splitting a log in twain as both pieces fell satisfyingly to the side of the stump he used to elevate the wood. He grabbed another log from the branch of a cherry tree found in the forest; they were easy enough for him to split quickly. Setting it on the log, he then took another full swing from around his back and into the log and the ax cracked through the wood and thudded itself in the stump.

"That'll be enough, March!" his father called to him. It was still early in the morning but the sun had risen enough to make its light supply enough heat so the boy would break a sweat after only a little work. He left the ax in the stump and gathered his split pieces onto two lines of rope, tied them and carried them to his father.

March noticed Alechi's father was still working, so he looked at his father and they agreed silently on what he should do. March retrieved his ax from the stump and approached Jerald, who was out of breath. The young boy motioned for the man to sit down and continued to chop until he was told to stop as they met the day's quota.

"Thank you, March," the friend's father told him.

He nodded in response then looked north. "Do you think he's coming back soon?"

"I hope so, the shaman was not clear on how long it would take him, so thank you again for helping me while he's gone."

"You're welcome. But I think when he gets back, we should make him help my dad, too."

Jerald laughed a little. "Maybe." He bound the piles of wood with rope and handed two to March. "Can you take these to my home? I'd like to visit Calius for a bit today."

"Absolutely." So March left and carried the wood to Alechi's house, the sneakiest and most efficient path still rooted in his memory as he took his strangely direct route through the village. It passed by Eliya's house and he thought again about stopping by and asking how she was doing. He had seen her out of her room, but she was still distant from all the others. He elected to pass for the day, as he had the day before, and every day for the last week. He saw Ezri tending to the family garden with some of the younger children standing to watch and learn. Dailyn saw March approach and used all the strength in her tiny body to open the door for him, pushing the door handle with her hands as high as they could above her head as if to prove a point. After he passed the threshold, the girl let the door close behind him and resumed her work outside.

He set the wood down next to the hearth and went back outside to greet Alechi's mother properly, but when he pulled the door he did not see anyone tending the garden. Before he could even think to wonder where they went, he noticed a commotion near the village center. A large wagon was stationed in the middle of the village. It had a circumscribed emblem with a large "T" and a treasure chest painted onto its fabric.

"A new merchant," March said, turning to go back to his home as his heart sank. He assumed one of the children had simply run off to the new merchant and their mother after them, nothing to concern himself with. Deciding that if he ever wanted to see what the new merchant offered, he would go when the commotion died down.

"March!" a familiar voice cried out from among the commotion.

When the sound reached his ears, March felt his heart well up. He looked and saw Alechi, surrounded by his family, waving his arms in large arcs to summon attention to himself. He said something quietly to his family, hugged each of them, and ran to March.

Alechi ran with all his might and March, as his friend approached, prepared for a harsh impact only to be met with a strong and tight hug. "I've missed you, March!" He said in their usual heroic voices they used whenever sparring.

Then responding using that same mockery of a deep voice, "And I've missed you, my brother!"

The pair laughed long enough for an inch of a shadow to grow. They both then grew serious, thinking their reasons to be separate, but discovering they were the same when March demanded to know why Alechi needed to go and Alechi explaining the answer to that very question.

He finished by saying, "And now, I have to finish the actusfie off once and for all. Tomorrow, my family and the shaman have already agreed to come and help, I am going to go to the open meadow outside the walls and destroy the actusfie." His heart was fully sincere as he made this request of his friend, "I would really appreciate it if you were there with me."

"I will on one condition: you let me hold your sword for a few moments."

Alechi chuckled as he unsheathed the blade blessed by Serinth and handed it pommel first to his friend. March examined the glinting blade in the sunset's rays and returned it to Alechi the same way he had received it. "Of course I'll help, but how are you going to get it out of you?"

"I have a few ideas."

As if-

"I can do it because Serinth, my family and you are all on my side, I have nothing to fear from it."

March was not clear on his role in the removal of the actusfie, but accepted that this was what his friend needed from him. The two then wandered about the village, discussing Alechi's adventures and the life in the village since he had been gone. Alechi told stories of the people he met and the beings he encountered, recounting with particular emphasis on the story of the drunk mercenary, Algoro, who had claimed to slay a dragon in the region. March noted how the name sounded familiar and realized it was the same man he had met and they laughed with each other at the mercenary's apparent lunacy. Then, in the midst of their conversations, deep night fell upon them. When they noticed at last how dark it had grown, the pair returned to their houses and agreed to meet in the morning.

When Alechi returned home, he found everyone else already asleep, albeit lightly as they shuffled a few inches upon his arrival. He lay down and thought of how he was to release the actusfie and Exsanai's question returned to him as to why he had gone out in the first place. Then a thought struck him, he meditated on it and on the words of the shaman who had explained the origins of the actusfie to him. Then content with what he had discovered of himself, he kept it in his thoughts as he drifted into sleep.

The next morning began, for Alechi, well after sunrise. When he awoke he found the house empty and realized everyone was doing their duties, including the ones intended for him he had hoped to resume upon his return home.

As he finished getting dressed for the day, his father came through the door.

"Why didn't you wake me up? I wanted to help, I told you that."

"That you did, but I happen to know it is no easy task to kill an actusfie and we figured we could let you sleep for today. You seemed tired."

"Oh," Alechi said, searching for any words to follow other than the one that came out of his mouth after, "thanks." He recalled Rorick's wisdom on resting and smiled.

"Shall we get going then? Everyone else is just about ready."

Alechi's mother was tending the garden with his siblings and when they saw him come out they stood, ready to follow him. March had been waiting nearby since he completed his regular morning duties and saw his friend leave the house. He waved to Alechi and joined the group gathering around his friend.

The group made their way to the shaman's house in the middle of the village, the small herd drawing some attention. The shaman saw them approach through his window and came outside to meet them. Standing next to the shaman were two people Alechi did not invite but was just as happy to see willing to help him: Calius and Tesvi. The shaman, the guard, and the merchant each greeted him with a firm handshake.

"Thank you for coming. All of you," Alechi said.

"Are you ready?" the shaman asked.

"As ready as I will ever be," he responded. "It will only get harder from now on, so if I don't think I'm ready now, I know I never will be." His response, while confusing to some of those in the group, was said confidently and brought a reassuring smile to the shaman's face.

"Lead the way."

Alechi led the pack of family and friends out the gate he had climbed over years ago and through the forest to the glade the rabbit had first met him in. And though he was unsure, he spotted the rabbit at the end of the tree line moments before it darted away deeper into the shrubs and wood around.

"I'll be back," Alechi said. He followed the rabbit as it led him to the cave where it all began. Fortunately, there was no bear, nor was it raining nor dark. The cave was before him, and for a moment he dared not enter.

I see you are still afraid. You should be if you think any of them can stop me. The actusfie made a noise that seemed like a mocking laugh.

In an act of defiance against the spirit, Alechi took a hard step forward into the cave. Alechi found the blue-flamed waters again, led by the rabbit, and dug up the cup he had buried so long ago with his hands.

Those were the days, don't you think? Why destroy it? Why not keep it? Why let go?

Alechi was familiar with these thoughts and their origin, so he sent them from his mind, an action of which the rabbit seemed to approve.

The pair, rabbit and boy, returned to the clearing where he had left his family and friends.

The shaman saw his return and began organizing the group. The boy went to the center where the rock was and stood in front of it. The shaman directed the others to form a circle around Alechi. He told them to close their eyes, limiting questions about the begemmed chalice Alechi carried, and think of Alechi as they knew him, praying to the axuli as they did. Once they were all in position and praying, the sheet-like feeling Alechi had described earlier felt even lighter and he knew the final step of the actusfie's release would be his own.

He took a few deep breaths to try and calm himself.

It's hopeless. You know that.

"All you do is lie," Alechi began, "you manipulate, you make me hurt my friends, my family and myself. You are not a part of me." He set the chalice on the stone.

Keep telling yourself that. Its laugh continued but shifted, it seemed to Alechi, more toward nervousness than confidence.

"I am loved by Serinth, by the axuli, I was made good, I desire good, I can change and I want to. You are jealous and desire only to hate, you don't want to change. You are not a part of me."

The actusfie made no comment and its laughing ceased. The sheet Alechi felt around him became looser as it began to tear.

The answer that came to him last night echoed in his mind and he passed it through his lips, "And I wanted you because I thought it would make me strong, I wanted to prove myself. I thought no one cared who I was. It was my foolish pride that made me go out and my fear that made me listen. I see now I don't need you. I never needed you," he looked at those who surrounded him. Then, closing his eyes, he said, "You are not a part of me, in the name of Serinth, get out." With a large swing from his sword, he struck the cup. It fell to the ground, shattering at the mere touch of the blade.

The illusory sheet felt like it tore violently, and wisps of black smoke accumulated in front of Alechi. The smoke continued to billow out from Alechi's chest silently becoming denser and denser. The smoke wrapped around the shattered pieces of the cup, picking them up as it formed into something.

The actusfie began to laugh maniacally and only then did Alechi reopen his eyes. Before him, protruding from his chest as the smoke continued to feed its body was a giant, winged serpent. A dragon.

17

Spring's Bloom

The dragon continued to grow before the boy. Its scales were pitch black and the dense smoke gave it also an ethereal appearance as its wingspan spread and began to shadow those around him. The ends of both wing was horned and a claw, formed from the metal of the chalice, topped each. Though they were hardly distinct, a pair of bright red eyes made of the gems from the chalice faded into view at the dragon's head. Wisps of smoke and pieces of shattered metal that seemed to form spikes along its spine were the only thing that broke the otherwise smooth body of the dragon. It had no other limbs than its wings and its size loomed over almost the entire glade.

As it had when they first met, the actusfie's voice was heard outside Alechi's own body; however, it said nothing as its laugh faded into a roar. It thrashed about in the sky and flapped its huge wings as it grew. A loud roar that could be heard for miles pierced the heavens and echoed throughout the forest all the way to Shre. It beat its wings hard as it separated at last from Alechi's body, attempting to rise even higher but then it seemed to hit some invisible barrier. It was sent hurling down a couple hundred feet before it regained itself and tried going in each direction but it was still caged. It could not leave the invisible dome that seemed to come from the loved ones around Alechi. The boy shook in his boots, wondering how none of the others were reacting to the giant beast before them and the noise it made.

Then, the shaman urged with a loud voice for everyone to tighten the circle around Alechi, possibly the most booming voice Alechi had ever heard him use. They each obeyed, taking careful steps with their eyes closed, relying on the shaman's voice to guide them. The circle shrunk and the invisible barrier's height shrunk with it. His friends, his family, his shaman were all there to help him win.

The dragon was trying its best, flying at high speeds, to attempt a break in the barrier but it was to no avail as the barrier shrunk it was brought closer to Alechi. It roared fearfully as it kept its distance from the blade Alechi bore.

When it at last became apparent to the simple dragon that it would not be able to escape, it started making attempts at Alechi. Alechi dodged and tried to swing, but he was too slow. Alechi grunted in frustration, but he thought of Will. *One more time.*

Another attack came as the dragon tail swept toward him. This time, Alechi was too early as he dodged and the tail struck him, sending him to the edge of the circle. Alechi was hurt.

The dragon made for a final gambit against the boy, diving straight for him with its jaws open wide with a terrifying roar, sure of its victory. Yet in that moment of potential doom Alechi regained his courage. *One more time! Get up!* He climbed to his feet, stood still, and silenced his inner thoughts, thinking back to the forge. He settled his heels into the stance he used so often for shoveling and waited. The dragon's straightforward attack backfired as Alechi used his shoveling stance and the practiced movement from the forge to bash its head with his buckler, stunning it. As the dragon remained dazed, Alechi slid on his feet to the top of the dragon's neck and swung the sword with all his might.

I can do it!

It did not pass through as easily as it had with the cougar actusfie in the woods, nor did the dragon instantly fizzle as the other beast had. Alechi had to struggle as the blade cut through the dense smoke as if it were a block of cold wax. He could not win the fight with his own power.

The dragon was regaining its strength.

He thought about the beast he and Tesvi fought just beyond the village. "Serinth, help me," Alechi said, when he realized he was only mere inches into the dragon's neck. "We have already won, please, just finish it."

Suddenly, an iridescent flame set his sword and buckler ablaze. The form of a giant, flaming bird erupted from the blade and engulfed the dragon. Then, as the flames from the sword were reabsorbed into the blade, Alechi saw a white stag enter the ring of his friends and family. The stag charged the dragon and pierced its side easily with its antlers, dragging the dragon's body back to the earth. "Serinth..." Alechi said in awe. The blade, aided by the antlers of the stag, began to make the smoke fizzle to dust. Alechi placed the shield on the dragon's head to keep it pinned down as he leveraged his body weight into pushing the blade down. Then at last, the blade passed through the smoke as though it were at last just that, smoke. When it had severed the neck, the dragon stopped moving. The ends where the blade had passed through burned steadily through the massive body like embers on the end of a paper. The ethereal smoke of the dragon faded to dust as it burned and fell to the earth.

The stag then removed its antlers and walked away, watching Alechi as it trod into the forest.

"Is that it?" Alechi asked. "Is it over?"

The stag offered no response.

"Thank you, everyone," the shaman said to the crowd. Then, as if to answer Alechi as the last of the dragon's dust was blown by the wind, he said, "You may open your eyes now. Your task is complete."

"What did we even do?" March asked, looking to either side for any change of environment. He heard none of the roars from the dragon, nor did anyone aside from the shaman and Alechi. Had they opened their eyes, they would not have seen the dragon either. The order to keep their eyes closed was for the sake of their own focus instead of being distracted by what would have only appeared to be a young boy slashing at the sky.

Alechi responded with the beginnings of a smile as he looked at all those around him, "You were here for me."

The season passed further through spring to the verge of summer. Tesvi had stayed for a few days to trade what he had and decided he would return someday for regular trade. And to see his friend. Otherwise, life seemed to have returned to normal for the little village of Lagdin.

It was time to hunt again so Alechi and his father gathered what they needed and went out early in the morning, leaving the responsibility of firewood to some of the other households that agreed to split the wood for their family.

Alechi brought the dagger his father had given him for the journey and kept it sheathed and strapped to his belt. The dagger had saved his life once with the help of Tesvi and now served, for him, as a memento of his journey that was far easier to carry than his sword and shield. It carried the weight of the memories he held in his heart.

"Here," his father said, handing him a bow. "I borrowed this from Calius yesterday and strung it for you. He said you could keep it as long as you promise to become as good as I am."

Alechi chuckled for a moment as he accepted the bow, "That will definitely take a while." It was a finely crafted and sanded ash wood bow that had a leather wrap for a grip around the center. He tested the weight of the draw string, barely managing to pull it all the way back before carefully relaxing it back to the bow.

"Better to start now then, isn't it? I'll make sure we get plenty today, so for now, let's make good use of those eyes of yours and get enough meat for a banquet!"

He let some air out of his nose, "A banquet? What for?"

"No reason." His father was never a talented liar, but Alechi decided not to press the question further.

They went to the eastern side of the village and began their hunt. They waited for some time, neither making a sound as they sat near the base of a tree in the deep woods looking past each other and glancing to either side to look for any antlers or tusks poking out. The hogs would migrate to this area at this time of year and supplied plenty of meat. Well worth the several arrows it took to take one down.

It took some time but Alechi spotted a pair of tusks in the distance and signaled to his father by putting his fingers to his mouth to imitate them. They walked heel to toe until they found themselves in the range of the hog. Jerald motioned for Alechi to take the first shot, so he draw his bow and aimed as carefully as he could and released the arrow. The arrow tore through the air but sank into the dirt a few feet to the right of the hog, which put it on high alert. He had another shot he could take before the hog would either run away or spot and charge them. He took a deep breath and aimed again brining his bow slightly higher and adjusting for the distance he missed with a few inches to the left. He loosed another arrow and it grazed the hog. It let out a small squeal then noticed the pair of hunters and started to charge at them. Jerald's limbs reacted fast as lightning as he loosed an arrow square into the hog's head. It ran for a few feet more before falling on its feet.

"Go get the arrows," Jerald commanded quietly.

Alechi nodded and managed to retrieve the arrow that had

grazed the hog, but the other arrow was too deep in the dirt for him to find.

"I guess we're down one then. Well two I should say," Jerald said. When the hog fell, its head bowed and broke the arrow as its head hit the ground. "Care to confirm it's dead?" Alechi pulled the dagger from its sheath and thrust the blade into the hog's neck, it did not even wince. "All right," his father said, "then let's get it back to the village."

They continued hunting all day and into the early hours of night and managed to kill a few more hogs, Alechi missing every shot he took yet getting closer to his target. As night was settling in, Jerald spotted their first stag.

The father nodded to his son who nodded back. He took a deep breath. The stag was crossing their range, so this was his broadest target for the day. He exhaled and loosed the arrow. The arrow landed in the stag's side, far from a deadly wound. The stag was taken off balance and lurched to the side, but it remained standing. It turned to face them and Jerald drew his arrow, ready to fire. The stag walked slowly toward them, its head held high in confidence. Jerald strengthened his draw. Alechi stared at the stag and it bowed its head to young man. "Let's leave this one alone," he said. He stepped toward the stag, removed the arrow from its side and the wound closed up instantly. Its color had not been clear in the darkness or the distance, but now he could see its white coat. Two deep holes penetrated its neck.

After the arrow was removed, the stag left and resumed its original path. It seemed it was going to make its way around the village, but it was getting too late for the hunters to pursue it any further. They returned to the village, checking and resetting the traps along the way, finding a few rabbits. They took the rabbits to the shaman and then home to use for another day.

The next day, after they had finished with their day's chores and the chores of some others, March and Alechi prepared to spar again in the village center.

"I am Alechi," the young man began his declaration, holding the stick he had for a weapon erect in the sky, "slayer of dragons! Who dares to challenge me?!" His weapon, the sword and buckler he had once carried along his journey, were never far away, but for the sake of fun and the safety of his friend, the stick seemed to be the appropriate downgrade.

"I do!" March cried out, boastful. "March, defender of Lagdin!"

Then with a battle cry from each of them, they charged at each other and landed nearly choreographed hits against the other's stick and pot lid. Their fight was reaching its end and March appropriately claimed his turn as the victor.

"Alas! I am defeated!" Alechi cried out. "Fair maiden, tell this mighty warrior to spare..." his voice faded as his eyes failed in their search of the village center for Eliya. "Oh," he said, guilt flooding his throat. "That's right."

March saw the pain in his heart and helped his friend to stand, throwing his weapon to the ground. "Come on," he said earnestly.

Alechi was familiar with the route from the center to Eliya's house and tried to protest when he realized it was where they were going. "March, I really don't think you understand how bad I hurt her."

"It's not my business to know exactly what you did, but it is my business, as both of your friends, to help you fix it." As they approached, they saw her outside, tending to the garden with her mother. "Eliya!" March called from a distance.

"Our fair-" Alechi began exaggeratedly in a last ditch effort to mask his own feelings from himself but it was met with a swift elbow to the side from March. "Hi, Eliya," he stammered out.

She stood and said nothing to either, but nodded to March. Her arms were crossed over her chest as she kept her distance while her mother watched from the side of her eyes.

"Alechi here has something he needs to say."

"I really am sorry about what I did. I've missed you a lot," realizing how his statement sounded, he rushed his next words, "I know the others miss you too." He then managed to collect himself again and said, feeling the words deep in his gut, "I'm sorry."

She looked back to her mother and to her house and for a few moments did not say anything to anyone. The pair read the signs and turned to leave.

"I did not want you to come back."

The boys paused, turning to face her again.

"I knew you were sorry the first time. I know you made a mistake, and I can forgive you for a mistake, but..." She took a breath, collected herself and continued, "I was hurt, okay? I did *not* want you to come back.

"Part of me wants to never see you again. March, I'm happy you get to have your friend again, but Alechi, you broke that boundary. You shattered everything. I can't know if you are ever going to do that again."

"Well that's the thing–!" March said, ready to tell her everything about the actusfie, yet for a reason unbeknownst to him, his friend stopped him.

"I may have been influenced by it, but I'm still responsible for what happened," he said to March. "She doesn't need excuses." Turning to Eliya, he asked, "What can I do to show you I'm the friend you used to know?"

"That's the problem... I don't think I ever knew you."

"I think you did. I lost myself for quite some time. What I did to you... I can't take it back and I can't change it. But I've found who I was. Who I was born to be. What can I do to help you believe me?"

Eliya fell pensive for a few moments. "There's nothing you can do. And even if there was... even if there was I don't know if I could trust that you aren't doing it as a trick. That you aren't doing it just because I said it would work."

Alechi wanted to protest but something reminded him of the actusfie. Silently, it dawned on him, *I was her actusfie.* He nodded a couple of times as his heart sank into his chest. "I understand," he said. "I hope I can be someone you can trust someday, but for now, I understand."

The pair left the girl's home and, upon reaching the village center, went their separate ways. Alechi returned to his family and helped prepare the dinner for the evening. A rabbit had been caught in the trap earlier in the day and taken to the shaman. Alechi reflected now on how there was always a rabbit for each family each day. He mixed each chunk of the rabbit one by one into a stew with the vegetables grown from their own garden with a new sense of reverence for the dish.

"Two gifts becoming one..." Alechi mused as he added the last of the chunks. No one in the family took notice of what Alechi had said, being too busy with one another and enjoying their own conversations. He smiled.

When the meal was finally ready, he prepared a bowl of the stew for each of his siblings and his parents, said a silent prayer of thanks to Serinth and ate with them. As they ate, they shared stories they had told each other at least a thousand times but still laughing at the same times as they always had. The settling of the fire settled the energy, but not the joy of the home. The calm coals' dim light reminded them of the quiet night beyond the walls of their home, and each, one by one, drifted into sleep.

Waking early the next morning, even before his father, Alechi went to chop wood. It was early enough that the light of the sun had not gone more than a few inches over the horizon, hinting at the dawn yet to come. He found the village to be peaceful in these early hours and with each swing of his ax he took a moment to wonder at the sky and the forest before him. Breathing in deeply through his nose, he closed his eyes and felt content with where he was. He was finding that even the simplest and most mundane of these labors was rewarding in its own right. He had finished chopping enough wood for his house's daily quota long ago but kept chopping to leave some for the others as they began to appear like fireflies at dusk. Scattered at first, then all at once.

Alechi offered the extra wood he chopped to March and his father before departing with the pile he had chopped for Calius' guardhouse. He paced himself through the village, stepping forward and backward, left and right as if he were dancing staring in wonder at the things he had seen countless times.

"Ahh! Alechi!" Calius said from the doorway, "Thank you as always for your help."

"It's my pleasure," Alechi said blissfully as climbed the steps and set the pile of wood by the door.

"Care to come inside?"

"Only if you'll have me."

Calius bowed his head slightly and waved his hand through the door as if guiding him along some mysterious path in his usual dramatic manner. The guard was smiling as he welcomed the young man. "It is a big day for you."

Alechi gave him a puzzled look and dismissed his comment as grandeur.

The other guards in the house welcomed Alechi inside and offered him some tea which he gratefully accepted. Like his own home, some thick blankets were spread along the side of the deep-set hearth which was burning low. The young man took the seat offered to him by the hearth. While there was hardly a need for additional warmth as spring continued to develop toward summer, the cool hours of the morning supplied a time when it could be considered necessary.

The guards discussed their general duties, strange things they thought they had seen near the outer walls, and sang the praises of the women they had come to love be it their mothers or their future spouse. Alechi shared another part of his journey with them as he had serialized the tale in speech with them every morning.

After some time, Jerald made an appearance at the guardhouse as well. He was greeted with another cup of tea and offered a seat next to his son. The conversations continued well past the sunrise but ended soon enough for family members to depart and help with the other duties around their home and the homes of other families.

When all the chores for the day seemed to be done, Alechi went to the center of the village to browse what the merchants, who began to arrive in packs starting a few days ago, had to offer while waiting for his friend to arrive. Nothing from the merchants piqued his interest, so he found a place to sit near the edge of the village center and took a moment to practice what he learned from Exsanai. He took a deep breath and closed his eyes.

After a while, his ears caught the sound of Casey and Dailyn playing nearby with their friends. It took them some time to notice him, but when they did, they bolted over to him.

"Come play Wolf and Sheep with us!" Casey said.

"Yeah, come on," Dailyn encouraged in her sweet voice.

"I don't know..." Alechi said, drawing out the last syllable and raising its pitch before letting it fall again. He was doing his best to hold a straight face which was enough to convince them that he was serious about not joining them. "What if I teach you a new game I learned in Som Catre?"

"Really?!" Casey begged. "Please?"

"Yeah, please?!" Dailyn said, joining in.

Alechi organized the children according to the game he played when he first met Will. He led the game much to the enjoyment his siblings and all the children gathered. The games continued until the legs of every child in the village were ready to fall out from underneath them.

March appeared shortly after they finished playing their game with plenty of daylight left to explore the forest and discover new hideouts. Then Alechi saw March's companion, one whom he did not expect: the shaman. The two left the shaman's home in the center, and much to the young man's surprise, the rest of his family began to appear in the center as well. He had expected them to be relaxing indoors with some of the other families. Jerald openly carried the sword and buckler that Serinth blessed and had slain the draconic actusfie.

Calius was not far behind. He was wearing his full set of steel armor, something very few guards ever felt the need to do, most finding it simpler to use their leather set. His well-conditioned, shining breastplate bore an emblem with antlers on it. He carried his longsword in a bright red scabbard on his left hip. He was almost unrecognizable.

Alechi stood eyebrows furrowed as he glanced his surroundings before the puzzle in his brain began to sort itself out.

"Alechi," the shaman began, "are you aware of what is about to happen?"

"I'm about to be assigned to a guardhouse, right?"

"Correct."

However, one last puzzle piece remained. "Am I even old enough?"

"It's not a matter of age," Calius said, rolling shoulders to stretch and pop his joints, "it's a matter of readiness." The shaman stared at the guard with a reproving gaze.

"And you think I am ready?"

"We all do," the shaman answered. "That is what I was just confirming with March. Each person here has attested to who you are: a hard-working, caring, kind, and respectful person fully capable of choosing others over himself. We have each seen you grow, Alechi, whether you've noticed it or not. For these things we deem you ready to begin an apprenticeship at a guard house until the time comes for you to fully join the guard and defend others in this village. Someday, you may lead your own and someday, you may lead this village. You may not be perfect now, but what matters is this: do you accept this commission to the guard house and pledge to continue to grow in your support of this village?"

Alechi searched his heart for a moment and found himself thankful: for the long journey behind him, and for the intense challenges of guard training ahead. In spite of the coming trials, he chose to think instead of the opportunity to join the guard. His qualification by the axuli, by Serinth. As he looked to his family and friends, they each gave him an approving nod, so he said, "I do."

Author's Note

As an author, there is only so much that I can do while leaving things open to interpretation. This is a story that spawned from a desire to answer certain questions for myself as I worked toward overcoming an addictive vice. I am Roman Catholic, and the idea for this book came to mind after my first in-person mass after the coronavirus pandemic began in 2020. I quickly typed up some notes in my phone and started working.

This book, I hope, has found its audience and has been generally applicable to many habitual vices, whether it is as simple as swearing or painful as pornography: an actusfie is any of these.

I have historically been deeply inspired by authors such as Tolkien and C.S. Lewis (really, what fantasy lover hasn't been inspired by them), and I wanted a book akin to *Lord of the Rings* where the reader could "hear" more of the inner turmoil of the individual like *The Screwtape Letters*. I like to think I accomplished my goal of offering others a way to reflect on themselves and help themselves while simultaneously giving their allies a better understanding of what may be passing through their minds.

There are a few things to note, however: first, is that this timeline is greatly reduced. For myself, this is an ongoing journey and this book is the amalgamation of everything I've learned, so if it doesn't take you only a few months after starting like it does for Alechi, fear not, you are not alone. The second may already have been apparent to some readers, but the moment you slay your own actusfie, whatever it may be, is not the moment of triumph, it is not the height of your story. That moment of triumph came when you decided to better yourself, when Alechi recognized his own desire to be better and rid himself of the actusfie. In other words, don't look for a "climax" in your own story of redeeming yourself. I remember receiving a comment about an earlier draft saying that the "climax" or final battle was "anti-climactic," and I agreed, but again, that was on purpose. The days I have found the most success are the days when I'm concerned with the vice the least. Don't give the actusfie the time of day. The last is this, Alechi faced many times where he felt alone, but it was after reflection he realized he was accompanied by axuli and kind people. Those who struggle with any vice often feel alone, but God walks beside you whether you know it or not: whether you believe it or not. — *David J. Neumaier*

Acknowledgements

The first recipient of my thanks is Jesus Christ. I got the idea for this story while I was sitting in my first in-person Mass since the start of the Covid-19 epidemic in 2020. Since then, the story has grown, honed, and helped me grow as a person. Without Jesus, I do not think this book would exist.

Second, I would like to thank everyone who supported me along the way. My friends, parents, spiritual directors, teachers, and family helped form the ideas and people that Alechi encounters. I would like to offer a particular thanks to my father for being a strong pillar of support in my development, particularly when it comes to my own shames and vices, as he walked with me, not above me.

Next, I would not have been able to write this book or have it developed from a title-less concept, to *Blessing*, and ultimately to *The Shadow and the Stag* without the help of Maria, Matthew, Kristen, Eli, and everyone who read sections or gave me feedback on even the smallest of ideas in passing conversation.

As of right now, I stand proud of this book even if it may still be incomplete. *The Shadow and the Stag* has been therapeutic to write, edit, and reread as it has helped me articulate and relearn lessons I have learned from others and my own experience.

Last, but certainly not least, I want to thank you, the reader for taking the time to read my book. It truly does mean a lot to have someone else read my work all the way through. I know this was a slower start than *Guardians of Aranor: Rebirth*, and I know some of you are waiting for that sequel, but I wanted to make sure people could read this story.

Thank you, and may the Lord bless you and keep you. May He guide your path and help you with whatever you may be struggling.